THE SPIRIT OF IRON EYES

The ruthless bounty hunter Iron Eyes is hot on the trail of the outlaw Diamond Back Jones. After running into the blazing guns of Jones's cohorts, Iron Eyes sees the deadly outlaw ride off into the arid Indian Territory. Wounded, Iron Eyes gives chase yet again but has no idea that he is being lured into a trap. The Apache are waiting to ambush the man they call 'the evil one'. Soon the bounty hunter finds himself facing a hundred painted warriors. But has he enough strength left to survive?

RORY BLACK

THE SPIRIT OF IRON EYES

Complete and Unabridged

LINFORD
Leicester

First published in Great Britain in 2004 by
Robert Hale Limited
London

First Linford Edition
published 2005
by arrangement with
Robert Hale Limited
London

British Library CIP Data

Black, Rory
   The spirit of Iron Eyes.—Large print ed.—
Linford western library
   1. Western stories
   2. Large type books
   I. Title
   823.9′14 [F]

ISBN 1–84617–051–6

Published by
F. A. Thorpe (Publishing)
Anstey, Leicestershire

Set by Words & Graphics Ltd.
Anstey, Leicestershire
Printed and bound in Great Britain by
T. J. International Ltd., Padstow, Cornwall

This book is printed on acid-free paper

*Dedicated to my oldest pals,
Tony, Phil and Pete Wall*

Prologue

Dry Gulch was a town that existed against all the odds. Hovering on the very edge of the vast untamed prairie which few white men had yet to venture into, it was the last place on earth that any sane man would visit. But outlaws shielded their sanity behind a multitude of vices and weaponry.

Dry Gulch provided a safe haven for hundreds of men and women who were not welcome anywhere else. It had long been said that even the Apache feared the vermin that filled its buildings and streets.

The blistering heat and blinding light from a sun which refused to yield to any season except high summer had shaped the land for hundreds of square miles above and below the Mexico border.

Those who rode into the remote Dry

Gulch were most probably loco or lost. Or both.

It had nothing for the faint of heart or honest souls. This was a town where gun law ruled supreme.

Yet it served its purpose.

It was one of the few settlements to have managed to take root in an otherwise arid landscape. It survived because it had to survive. There was no alternative. The buildings were mostly adobe and whitewashed like so many south of the border. A few wooden structures had been built by newer residents even though the imported wood was already being destroyed by a never-ceasing heat. At least half the inhabitants were of Mexican origin, but even they seemed to feel the unbelievable temperature hard to cope with as they took refuge within the boundaries of the town.

Only rattlers could ever be comfortable here.

Dry Gulch was indeed unlike any other place that Iron Eyes had ridden into, but he was here for a reason. He was hunting the bounty on an outlaw's head and nothing could stop him from the chase. His cold calculating eyes studied everything around him as he steered the Indian pony through the wide dusty streets and aimed for the large adobe building with the most horses tied up outside.

He knew that only places that sold either hard liquor or female company attracted that many horses in any town. He guided the pony with the thin bony fingers of his left hand whilst resting his right wrist on top of one of the Navy Colts tucked into his belt.

The saloon had its name marked on the side wall in paint that had long since lost its battle with the hot sun. What was left of the flaking red colour was illegible.

A few curious people had ventured out into the bright sunlight to watch the strange-looking rider pass them. None posed any threat to the lethal bounty hunter.

Iron Eyes shook the long limp hair off his face to reveal the scars of many previous battles. His skin was tight to the skull, which looked as if it belonged to a dead man and not a still-living person.

He reined in and glanced along the line of mounts who had been left in the blazing sun. His eyes darted at the ground and studied the hoof tracks behind the hind legs of the abandoned mounts. Instinctively he recognized the tracks that he had trailed for days. The dried lather on the buckskin mount also told him that he had found his prey at last.

Iron Eyes looped his right leg over his pony's neck and slid to the ground. He dropped his reins and allowed the tired mount to walk to the closest trough in search of water. He pushed his way between the horses and stepped up on to the raised boardwalk outside the adobe saloon.

He lowered his head until his chin touched the sweat-soaked shirt-collar, then stared at the dark interior of the saloon before him.

A hundred smells filled his flared nostrils. He ignored them all except the one he recognized as belonging to the man he had chased for so long.

Iron Eyes strode confidently into the saloon. It was slightly cooler in the large interior but he did not notice. All he could think about was finding the man whose image was on the wanted poster inside his deep coat pocket.

More than fifty people were crammed into the building. He could not even see the bar, but knew that it had to be directly ahead of him because that was where the most men were gathered as they fought for whiskey. The floor was covered in straw and a multitude of other less pleasant things.

Only those closest to the tall fearsome figure noticed the presence of the stranger in the noisy saloon. Iron Eyes opened the front of his long coat to reveal the jutting grips of his Navy .36s.

Slowly the crowd began to move away from him as it dawned on them that this stranger was here not to drink, but to kill. It was etched in every scar that covered Iron Eyes' face.

The bounty hunter began to walk forward with deliberate steps. He was silent and yet totally aware of all those who surrounded him within the crowded building. His fingers flexed as his arms hung at his sides. Only his spurs made any sound as he crossed the filthy floor.

His bullet-coloured eyes darted from one face to another, with a speed that only those who lived by their instincts could ever match. Iron Eyes inhaled deeply and followed the acrid scent of the man he had been chasing for so long. He turned his head and looked over the dozens of hats towards a far corner.

It was dark there but he could smell the outlaw drifting on the cigar and pipe-smoke-filled air.

Fear stank and Iron Eyes knew the aroma well.

Iron Eyes raised his left hand and brushed men aside as he moved closer to the darkest part of the large room. He was being drawn like a moth to a flame towards the outlaw he had yet to see.

Then he saw a brief glimpse of daylight as the saloon's rear door was hastily opened and closed. Diamond Back Jones had fled.

The sound of the door bouncing against its frame echoed above the drunken voices which filled the large room.

Iron Eyes increased his pace. He flung every one of the men between the corner of the saloon and himself out of the way as he closed in on the still moving door.

'Who you pushin'?' one man snarled as he grabbed at the sleeve of the bounty hunter.

Iron Eyes turned his neck and then brutally head-butted the far shorter man on the bridge of his nose. Blood splattered from the deep gash as the man fell to the ground.

Without pausing for a single second, Iron Eyes raised his right leg and kicked at the frail wooden door. It flew off its hinges and landed out in the sun-drenched alley.

Sunlight swept into the saloon but Iron Eyes did not seem to notice as he walked out into the alley. His nose was still guiding him after the man whose stench had drifted on the air between them for days.

The sound of Jones running filled his ears.

The thoughtful bounty hunter pulled a long thin cigar from his deep pocket, bit off its tip, then spat it out. He placed the cigar between his small teeth and then found a match. He ignited it with his thumbnail, cupped the flame and puffed until smoke billowed from his mouth.

Iron Eyes looked down at the ground and saw the bootmarks in the sand. They led along the narrow alley towards the backs of more adobe buildings.

'Keep running, Diamond Back,' Iron Eyes muttered through the smoke. 'I'm comin' and there ain't no hole deep enough for you to hide in.'

The bounty hunter walked between the high walls along the alley. He knew that he now had his prey running scared and that suited him. Above all other things, he was a hunter. It had once been animals, now it was men with prices on their heads whom he tracked down and killed.

There was a fork in the alley about a hundred feet from the rear of the saloon. The ground was baked hard by the merciless sun and there were no boot tracks to be seen by normal eyes, but there was no hiding-place from Iron Eyes' expert vision. He went to the right and continued his search.

Suddenly he heard a noise ahead of him.

Iron Eyes dragged one of his guns from his belt and cocked its hammer. He moved silently along the alley and stopped when he saw Diamond Back

Jones's boots disappearing over a wall. He went to aim, but his target had vanished.

The bounty hunter headed quickly towards the wall, then heard the outlaw running away from it across the hard ground. He stretched up to his full height and stared over the top of the whitewashed wall. He saw Jones race between two buildings and into a street.

The outlaw was heading back to his horse.

Iron Eyes gritted his teeth and ran along the alley in the direction of the street. A trail of blue smoke drifted over his broad shoulders as his long legs ate up the ground beneath him.

Before the tall man reached the street, he saw Diamond Back Jones dash across the mouth of the alley ahead of him.

Iron Eyes dragged his other pistol from his belt and readied it for action. As he reached the corner, the deafening sound of a shot bounced off the solid walls. When Iron Eyes stepped out into the street the wall exploded next to his face when a score of bullets hit it.

Debris showered over the bounty hunter as another volley of bullets passed within inches of the tall man's head.

Iron Eyes dropped on to one knee and returned fire as more shots rang out from the direction of the saloon.

Looking up, he saw at least a dozen gunmen fanning their gun hammers as they gave cover to the notorious Diamond Back Jones.

Iron Eyes rolled over and over back towards the alley as the ground all around him was churned up by the deadly bullets which sought his emaciated frame.

He returned fire and watched one of the gunmen drop lifelessly into the sand.

More shots echoed around Dry Gulch. They ricocheted off the wall behind him sending clouds of choking dust covering the kneeling man.

Iron Eyes rubbed his face and

11

squinted. He saw as Diamond Back was given a fresh mount and galloped off beyond the firing gunmen.

'Damn!' Iron Eyes cursed as he fired back again at the men.

One man twisted on his high heels and fell under the hoofs of the tethered mounts as one of Iron Eyes' bullets hit him squarely in the chest. Then another man strode out of the saloon with a double-barrelled shotgun in his hands.

Before Iron Eyes could cock the hammers of his guns again, he saw the long barrels blast out in his direction. A massive chunk of whitewashed adobe was severed from the side wall of the building above him.

It fell heavily on top of the bounty hunter's head.

Iron Eyes felt a crippling pain inside his skull as the heavy debris forced his face into the dust.

For a split second, everything went black in the mind of the prostrate figure. He then heard the muffled sound of boots behind him in the alley.

Somehow he managed to turn on to his side and stare at the alley.

His blurred eyes tried to focus. Then he saw two men rushing at him with their guns cocked and ready.

The men started to fire at the stunned figure. The deafening noise and blinding flashes of gunfire ripped through the alley and blasted at the ground next to him.

Iron Eyes' left hand plucked one of the Navy Colts off the ground and aimed at them.

With all his strength he dragged back the hammer with his thumb and then squeezed its trigger. He repeated the action three times more until he was convinced that the gunmen were either dead or wounded.

Then bullets rained down on the bounty hunter again from the saloon. He felt blood trickling down from his hairline as one of the gunmen's shots burned through his hair.

Iron Eyes rolled over again and faced what was left of his attackers.

There were about eight of them as far as his dazed eyes could tell. Yet Iron Eyes knew that he was hurt and not hitting his targets. The figures were swaying and blurred.

'Get him, boys!' A voice rang out as more shots came searching for the bounty hunter.

Iron Eyes knew that Jones must have paid these men to buy him time. Time the outlaw needed to get away. Time to put a lot of distance between himself and the legendary hunter of men.

He raised himself up on to his knees and aimed the barrels of his deadly guns at the men. Yet he could not tell if his eyes were lying to him. It was like looking through a heat haze even worse than the one which already filled the streets of Dry Gulch.

As each of the gunmen fired, Iron Eyes fired at the sound their pistols were making.

He saw men spinning and falling as his bullets slowly began to find their targets.

Then he saw the man with the shotgun again.

Iron Eyes blasted at the man with both Navy Colts.

The shotgun went flying into the air as the man was hit off his feet. A spray of blood splattered across the saloon's whitewashed frontage.

'Who is that *hombre*?' one of the gunmen screamed out from across the street.

'Diamond Back said he was a bounty hunter!' another voice answered from beside the line of skittish mounts.

'A bounty hunter? He ain't even human!' another man yelled.

'Damn right I ain't!' Iron Eyes snorted under his breath as he opened the chambers of his red-hot guns.

Iron Eyes emptied the spent shells from his guns, then filled their chambers with bullets from his deep pockets. As he slid the last of the bullets into the Navy Colts, he rose to his full height and spat the twisted cigar from his lips.

'Ready or not, I'm comin',' Iron Eyes shouted as he walked towards the startled onlookers.

There was an astonished gasp from the men who faced him.

With blood streaming down his grotesque face he fired both weapons in unison. The long tails of his coat flapped violently as the gunmen's shots missed his painfully thin body and tore at the weathered blood-stained fabric.

Shot after shot spewed from the barrels of his Navy .36s as the bounty hunter advanced on his attackers. His flared nostrils could smell their terror.

With every step of his long legs, Iron Eyes saw the men buckle as his deadly bullets tore into them.

By the time the dazed gaunt figure reached the line of terrified horses outside the saloon, Iron Eyes knew that he had killed them all.

There was blood everywhere across the bright dust. It traced between the twisted bodies that lay all around him. His eyes narrowed and stared at the dust that hung on the hot air, marking the trail left by the fleeing Diamond Back Jones.

Iron Eyes tucked one pistol into his belt, leaned against the saddle of one of the horses and then looked up at the saloon and the frightened faces in the darkness.

He produced a golden eagle from one of his pockets and tossed it into the saloon's dark interior.

'Whiskey!' Iron Eyes growled as blood dripped from his limp hair. 'Somebody better get me a few bottles of whiskey! I got me an outlaw to trail and kill.'

1

The blazing heat was as merciless as the rider who forced his exhausted pony through it. Standing in his stirrups, the horseman continued to whip his long reins across the shoulders of the pitiful animal beneath him. The tails of his long bloodstained coat flapped over the cantle of his saddle as his long black hair moved up and down on his back like the wings of a bat seeking the sanctuary of a distant cave.

The chase had started again.

The blood had dried on his scalp an hour earlier but Iron Eyes had already forgotten the wound which had almost cost him his life in Dry Gulch far behind him.

He had a crumpled wanted poster buried in his deep coat pocket, amid countless loose bullets. The bounty hunter had trailed his prey for nearly a week before he had reached Dry Gulch.

Somehow Diamond Back Jones had managed to escape.

Now Iron Eyes was forced again to trail his prey. He could see nothing except the tracks on the prairie floor before his exhausted pony.

Mile after mile he had followed the outlaw until he had reached this remote inhospitable place. Yet Iron Eyes did not seem to notice that the land itself was now becoming as much an enemy as the unseen rider far ahead of him.

The hoof-tracks led straight on across the blindingly bright terrain. They were luring him like bait and he knew it. Yet he would not stop following Jones. Not now. Not after he had been so close to collecting the price on his head back in Dry Gulch.

The sight before him would have terrified any normal man, but not this deadly creature. He feared nothing.

The bullet-coloured eyes had never lit upon anything which gave them reason to doubt his own deadly ability with his matched pair of Navy Colts. For death had ridden on his shoulder for his entire life and he knew that there was a time for all things to die. He would accept his own fate when it came, but not give his enemies an easy target.

Apache war smoke drifted up from beyond the distant sea of sagebrush. It twisted into the cloudless blue sky and hung there for knowing eyes to read its dark ominous message.

Iron Eyes could not read the message in the smoke but knew it had to be about either Jones or himself.

The sun-baked prairie was one place where the notorious bounty hunter did not want to get cornered by anyone, especially the Apaches who ruled this seemingly barren land. Iron Eyes wondered why the outlaw had headed straight into such a dangerous place at all.

Iron Eyes drew in his reins, stared up at the smoke and squinted hard into the distance. He ran his long bony fingers through his lank matted hair and growled angrily.

Whatever the smoke said, he knew it had something to do with his being in the middle of Apache land. The Indians had spotted him following the trail left by the outlaw from the sand cliffs which edged the entire prairie.

He reached back to one of his saddle-bag satchels and flicked the metal fastening open. He dragged out a full bottle of whiskey and raised its neck to his razor sharp teeth.

Iron Eyes pulled the cork from the black glass and spat it at the sandy ground. The aroma of the cheap liquor filled his nostrils a second before he curled his scarred lips around the bottle neck.

He swallowed hard, then lowered it and sighed heavily.

His thin neck turned as his keen eyes studied every inch of the horizon which surrounded him.

Then he saw them.

There were two other plumes of

black war smoke behind him. One to the east and the other to the west. It became obvious to the gaunt skeletal figure that the Indians ahead had been warned of his intrusion into Apache territory by the smoke signals far behind him.

They had spotted him hours earlier and by now, Iron Eyes suspected that probably every one of the tribe knew that the man known to them as the living ghost was almost within range of their rifles and bows.

Iron Eyes hated the Apache even more than he hated most living creatures. They were brave. Too brave. In all his many encounters with their various peoples, he had always been badly injured whenever they ran into one another.

He had killed many men in his time and a lot of them had been Indians. But he only hunted and killed white men for the price on their heads. The Apache were different. They usually attacked him and that annoyed the tall rider.

There was no profit in killing anyone for free.

The bounty hunter adjusted the two lethal pistols whose grips jutted from his belt above the buckle. As always, they were loaded and ready for action.

The cold eyes glanced again at the war smoke ahead of him as he sipped at the whiskey thoughtfully.

He started to wonder how many Apache were out there beyond the sagebrush.

A hunting party?

Somehow he doubted it. Every ounce of his being told him that there were far more Apaches ahead of him than he had ever had the misfortune of meeting before.

He searched amongst the bullets in his coat pocket and pulled out the grubby poster and stared at it hard. The crude photographic image was not clear enough to be certain, but Iron Eyes began to wonder if Diamond Back Jones might not be part Indian himself.

Could that be why the deadly outlaw

had led the bounty hunter here?

Was Diamond Back actually an Apache?

The thought nagged at the tall man.

Was he now the hunted and no longer the hunter?

Had Diamond Back Jones turned the tables on him?

Iron Eyes stepped off the pony and continued taking mouthfuls of whiskey as he walked around his lathered-up mount. No matter how much liquor he swallowed, he could not rid his mouth of the bitter taste that lingered.

He knew that there was no safe way out of this land.

Iron Eyes had been drawn into a well-laid trap.

2

From the sandy ridge the outlaw focused his binoculars on Iron Eyes far below on the prairie floor. Diamond Back Jones stood amid the hundred or more Apache braves watching the solitary figure who was standing beside the pitiful pony, drinking his whiskey. He lowered the glasses and glanced across at the stone-faced Apache chief Conchowata.

'Iron Eyes!' Diamond Back Jones said in an almost triumphant way. 'I told you that I would bring the evil one here, great chief. Didn't I?'

'You did, my brother,' Conchowata agreed. 'You have fulfilled your promise to your people. When you went to learn the ways of the white eyes, I thought they would destroy you as they have destroyed everything Apache. But I was wrong.'

'He looks a little confused.' The smile that had graced Jones's face for more than an hour grew wider with every passing heartbeat.

'The one known as Iron Eyes must be mighty scared!' the chief grunted forcefully.

'I don't think Iron Eyes has ever been scared in his whole life, Conchowata,' Diamond Back Jones said as he handed the binoculars to the painted Apache chieftain. 'Take a closer look at his face through them glasses.'

Conchowata narrowed his eyes and looked through the small eye-pieces at Iron Eyes. His fingers turned the small metal wheel until the focus was crystal clear. He studied the bounty hunter's scarred face carefully. The Apache was stunned by the sight. He had never imagined that anyone could look quite so horrific.

'Iron Eyes has been in many battles. He wears his victories on his face.'

Diamond Back rubbed his smooth chin thoughtfully. 'What do you think he is, great chief? Mexican? White or Indian?'

The Apache warrior brooded over the question.

'He not like any other men I have seen before. He not even look alive.'

'He's alive OK.' Jones nodded. 'I seen him bleed. Ya gotta be alive to bleed.'

Conchowata noticed the whiskey bottle in the bounty hunter's hand. 'Look! Iron Eyes drink fire-water!'

'They reckon the varmint lives on the stuff,' Jones informed the Indian. 'But they say he never gets drunk. No matter how much fire-water he drinks, he never gets drunk.'

The chief patted the outlaw's shoulder.

'You did good, my brother. You have lured the living ghost into the land of the Apache just like you said you would. At last we shall get our revenge.'

The outlaw removed his Stetson and shook his head. The long black hair fell on to his shoulders.

'I have never forgotten that I am an Apache, Conchowata. I have lived with the white eyes for many moons and learned their ways. But I am like you. I am Apache.'

The chief stared through the binoculars at the distant figure and smiled.

'Iron Eyes has been curse to our people for many moons. He shall pay for all the crimes he has committed against us. Now it will be him who is hunted like a dog.'

Diamond Back nodded as he stared into the blinding sun without blinking.

'This is a good day for our people. We shall kill the evil one who has taken the lives of so many of our brothers. We shall drink his fire-water and give thanks to the Great Spirit.'

Conchowata returned the black binoculars to Jones and began to walk through his heavily painted braves towards their mounts.

'We will kill Iron Eyes very slowly. We shall strip the flesh from his bones and feed it to our camp dogs. He shall suffer the death he deserves. A thousand knife-points will make him loco. Then we will make him beg us to end his agony. He shall know the vengeance of the Apache before he travels to the happy hunting ground.'

Diamond Back walked next to the chief as the rest of the Apache braves followed them to the line of horses. He had known that bringing the living ghost to his tribe would ensure his safe passage through the land that he had grown up in. A land that had taught him to survive.

But unlike the rest of his kind, Diamond Back had wanted more than the Apache life could ever give him. He had seen how the white men lived and the luxuries they enjoyed. That was his idea of living. He wanted to walk into a café and have money to buy an inch-thick steak covered in gravy. Being a ruthless outlaw had given him that. Diamond Back Jones knew that he would never again search for grubs to eat like the rest of his tribe. To be only one day away from starvation held no romantic for value him.

Diamond Back had tasted the fruits of the white eyes.

He liked it.

But being an outlaw brought dangers. The worst of which was the mysterious Iron Eyes. A man who seemed neither white nor Indian. A bounty hunter who it was said could never be killed because he was already dead.

Jones rubbed his chin again as he and the rest of the Apache reached their mounts. Without Iron Eyes hunting him, he could probably continue his killing and stealing until he was too old to raise a gun in his hand.

Leading the notorious bounty hunter here had achieved two things. It had raised his profile with the people he had abandoned and ensured that he always had a place where he could hide out from the law. It had also put the one man he feared in deadly danger. He knew that even Iron Eyes could not get out of this situation alive.

Without the most feared bounty hunter on his trail, Jones could continue on to Texas and start killing and robbing again until he had everything he desired.

Not that he had ever managed to get quite enough of anything he wanted. For killing had an addictive quality and he never seemed to be satisfied with any amount of stolen money.

'We go and capture Iron Eyes!' Conchowata shouted to all his braves.

Every one of the painted warriors threw himself on the back of his pony and began to make war cries to the cloudless sky above them.

Mounting his horse, the Apache outlaw known as Diamond Back Jones tried to stop smiling.

It was impossible.

3

Iron Eyes could feel the sand beneath his mule-ear boots moving long before he heard the spine-chilling sound of the Apache war cries. Any normal man would have been terrified. But not the bounty hunter.

'Damn Apaches!' Iron Eyes grumbled under his breath. He ran a match across his saddle and brought its flame to the tip of the mangled black cigar remnant. He sucked in the acrid smoke and then blew the flame out. 'I hate damn Apaches! They just can't leave me be.'

He tossed the match away, looked at his pony and knew that it had little strength left after the merciless punishment he had inflicted upon it since he had been trailing the outlaw Jones.

'Get ready, horse. I'm gonna push you 'til ya drop.' Iron Eyes lifted the bottle to his mouth and finished its contents.

His cold eyes focused across the sagebrush. The hunter of men could see the dust starting to rise as the Indians got closer. He inhaled the last of the smoke from the cigar and then flicked it away angrily.

'There sure looks like there's a lot of them this time,' he muttered.

He tossed the empty bottle aside and stepped into his stirrup. With one fluid movement, Iron Eyes mounted the pony and gathered up the loose reins in his bony hands. Now he could see the painted faces screaming in the blazing heat. There was still no fear in him, only frustration.

'Damn! Looks like the whole Apache nation has come to visit me this time, horse.'

This was the one territory that he hated. It was filled with dozens of creatures that seemed to have no other purpose than killing people. They either stung, bit or ate their prey. But of all the things to be found in this devilish inferno, it was the Apache he loathed the most. Most Indians he had met over the years would let him pass through their lands, but not the Apache. They liked to fight and they were too darn good at it for the bounty hunter's liking.

This territory was swarming with several different Apache tribes, each as deadly as the next. He had encountered most of them during his life and had the scars to prove it.

Iron Eyes ignored the approaching warriors and allowed the skittish mount to turn full circle slowly as he squinted out across the rest of the arid terrain.

The heat haze made everything appear to be moving like water flowing from a high cliff before his eyes. He then stopped the pony and stood in his stirrups.

For a brief moment Iron Eyes thought that he had seen something out there far beyond the sandy ridges which surrounded the prairie. He held the pony in check and stretched to his full height. He screwed up his eyes and

35

forced them to search for a place where he might find cover.

'I ain't too sure what that is out there, but I'll never find out hanging around here,' Iron Eyes told himself.

The sound of the approaching Indians became louder and louder as the rider kept staring out into the swirling heat haze. The sound of rifles being fired rang out across the flat landscape but he ignored it as he continued to stare at the distant object.

Was there something out there?

Iron Eyes knew that the prairie could fool even the wisest of souls. Make a man see lakes where there was only burnt sagebrush. It had the power to convince the unwary that there were solid structures where in reality there was only shimmering hot air.

He knew that the chances of reaching anywhere that he might be able to use for cover were remote but Iron Eyes had to try and find sanctuary somewhere.

Bullets hit the ground a mere dozen

yards from where his pony was standing, kicking up plumes of sand as the riders drew closer.

'Easy, horse!' the bounty hunter told his pony, holding the reins tightly in both hands.

Iron Eyes turned his thin neck to his right and looked through the long limp strands of hair that fell over his face. He could now make out the painted faces of the Apache horsemen galloping straight at him.

There were far more of them than he had ever witnessed in any one place at one time before.

They were riding towards him. It was like a wall of living colour. Rifles were cocked and fired along the entire length of the screaming warriors.

He felt the heat of a bullet pass within inches of his face.

'Reckon it's time to go, horse!' Iron Eyes sat down on his saddle and jabbed his sharp spurs into his pony's flesh.

The animal bolted.

The tall thin figure allowed the pony

to find its own pace as he continued looking at the wall of Apache riders who were closing in on him.

Iron Eyes hauled his reins to his left and spurred again. He had to try and put distance between himself and his deadly pursuers.

He stood up in his stirrups again and whipped the shoulders of the exhausted pony with the ends of his long reins as he balanced a few inches above the saddle. Holding the reins in his left hand he drew one of his Navy Colts from his belt and cocked its hammer.

With his arm outstretched, he aimed and fired again and again at the wall of Indians.

The sand beneath the pony's hoofs was becoming softer and slowing the tired mount's progress as its master tried to urge it on.

Iron Eyes knew that he could take most of his weight off his mount's back if he were to lean over its neck. He balanced as far forward as he dared.

'C'mon, horse! Get moving. You

don't want them Apaches to catch us, do ya? They'll kill me, but they'll eat you!' Iron Eyes yelled into the pony's ear.

The pony somehow found more speed and started to gather pace as its rider switched guns and continued firing at their attackers.

Iron Eyes gritted his teeth and held on to his saddle horn as the pitiful animal continued to gallop. The sound of shots was almost deafening as more and more of his pursuers managed to fire their rifles at him.

The air was alive with rifle bullets passing above and behind him. Iron Eyes whipped the pony again and then looked ahead and saw the sandy ridge was now getting tauntingly closer with every stride of his pony.

He narrowed his eyes and squinted through the swirling heat haze at the ridge of sand-coloured rock. He saw a black triangle shape half-way up the golden rockface.

Was it a cave?

His mind raced.

This was no mirage, Iron Eyes thought.

Whatever it was, it was real.

But there was no time to get excited. The sound of the Indians was growing louder and louder as they gained on him.

'C'mon, horse!' The words had barely left his dry cracked lips when he felt the animal beneath him shudder under the impact of a rifle bullet.

The sound which came from the animal instantly told Iron Eyes that his mount had been hit by one or more of the Apache riders' bullets.

The bounty hunter hit the ground hard and rolled like a tumbleweed when the wounded pony collapsed. He got to his feet and continued to run towards the sandy ridge. With every step, his skilled hands emptied the spent cartridges from his weapons and reloaded them with bullets from his deep coat pockets. The sound of the Indian ponies grew louder as shots rained all around him.

Iron Eyes tripped and fell. He swung around on the sand and narrowed his eyes before cocking both gun hammers and firing the Navy Colts.

'I hate damn Apaches!' he growled.

4

Iron Eyes blasted each of his Navy
Colts in turn at the scores of riders who
were driving their painted ponies ever
closer. He did not wait to watch the
Apache braves falling off their mounts
as his deadly bullets found their targets.
The bounty hunter realized that the
almost flat prairie offered him no cover
from the rifle bullets and arrows of his
enemies. Dodging the lethal projectiles
he ran back to his fallen pony. He
dropped behind the back of the stricken
horse and pushed his shoulder up to
the saddle. Bullets ripped up the
ground and showered sand all over him
as he continued to fire his matched
.36s.

The critically wounded pony was still
kicking aimlessly at the hot air as blood
poured from the three neat bullet holes
in its side.

There was no emotion in the gaunt features of the fearless Iron Eyes. He swiftly reloaded his guns again and resumed firing at the yelling Apaches. Bullets tore into the padded leather saddle behind the head of the cornered man. Every impact made the pony whinny as it vainly tried to get off the blood-soaked sand.

Iron Eyes had already managed to shoot more than a dozen of the avenging Indians, but he knew that there were still roughly ninety more heading straight at him. An arrow landed less than three inches from his groin between his painfully thin legs but he still did not seem to take any notice. He continued squeezing the triggers of his guns and watching his accurate bullets knocking the horsemen off the backs of their mounts. But there was no emotion on his face.

No hint of what the trapped man was thinking as he blasted his foes with the Navy Colts. He was killing because men were trying to kill him. It was as simple as that.

Again, his guns were empty.

Iron Eyes' fingers searched his deep jacket pockets for more ammunition.

'Damn!' Iron Eyes cursed.

He was running low on the precious .36-calibre bullets. He rolled over to the saddle-bags. The aroma of whiskey from the crushed bottles filled the hot prairie air. Iron Eyes dragged the top satchel off the bleeding horse and tore its buckle from the leather body of the bags. Two cardboard boxes of bullets fell on to the damp liquor-soaked sand.

Feverishly the bounty hunter pulled the cardboard lids off the boxes and emptied their contents into his pockets. Suddenly an another arrow came out of the gunsmoke filled air and hit the pony in the neck.

A spurt of steaming blood arced into the air. There was a gushing sound as air escaped from the deep wound.

Iron Eyes cocked his hammers and pushed his tall frame up as close to the dead animal as he could. The Apache were starting to circle the bounty hunter's dead horse. Dust rose off the unshod hoofs and mixed with the gunsmoke that hung on the hot prairie air.

Within seconds Iron Eyes could not see them and they could not see him.

For the first time since the painted warriors had given chase, Iron Eyes felt that he might just have a chance of surviving their relentless attack.

The dust from the ninety or more horses was blinding. The Apache braves continued to fire their bows and rifles but their target could no longer be seen.

He ignored the relentless volleys of bullets and arrows that came at him from all directions and raised himself up off the sodden sand. The animal's blood covered most of his coat and right trouser leg but he neither noticed nor cared. He threw his lean frame over the saddle.

Iron Eyes landed on his boots and

45

blasted both his pistols before stooping and running under the smoke and dust. He paused and listened to snorting Apache mounts approaching him from his left.

He ducked even lower and stared into the choking dust.

His keen eyesight could make out dozens of horses' legs as their masters twisted and turned them in vain attempts to locate their elusive prey.

Rifle shots cut through the smoke and dust from the Apache rifles above his head. Red-hot tapers of lead traced through the air but Iron Eyes did not move a muscle.

Again he moved like a mountain lion closer to the scores of bareback riders who were continually circling the area.

Unseen and unheard, Iron Eyes paused briefly and cocked the hammers of his guns once more. Again he fired up into the swirling smoke and heard the muffled cries as his bullets found their invisible targets.

He rested on one knee. His dust-caked eyes tried to find a solitary rider, apart from the bulk of the screaming braves, whom he could surprise.

Iron Eyes knew that he needed a horse, and was determined to get one.

Suddenly the legs of a pinto came into view from his left. He could see its master's moccasins hanging at the side of the pony. The eerie sound of arrows being unleashed from a bow whispered above the bounty hunter as he edged closer towards the pony's legs. Iron Eyes slid both guns into his deep pockets and then pulled his Bowie knife from the neck of his boot.

Again he moved closer until he was right under the snorting pinto's neck. He reached up and caught hold of the rope that was looped through its mouth.

Iron Eyes released his grip on the crude bridle and then swung around through the choking smoke and dust to face the Indian bowman. With the speed and agility of a puma, the tall ghostlike figure reached up and pulled the Apache towards him. The long lethal blade of the knife was thrust into the Indian's chest as he was dragged off the pony.

Before the lifeless body crashed to the ground, Iron Eyes had grabbed the mane of the pony and thrown himself on to the back of the confused animal.

Iron Eyes turned the pony and was suddenly confronted by a half-dozen Apache riders.

Even through the thick dust, the bounty hunter could see the stunned expressions etched into their painted faces. He drove his spurs into the pinto and charged straight at them. He lashed the deadly blade to one side and then the other as he forced his mount to ride straight through their ranks.

Blood dripped off the Bowie knife's gleaming blade as Indians fell all around the determined horseman.

When at last he had carved his way into the clear, Iron Eyes drove the Apache pony on towards the sandy ridge.

The pinto pony thundered across the

flat ground as it felt its new master's long, sharp spurs driving into its flesh. Yet no matter how fast it galloped, it could not escape the ruthless pain that Iron Eyes continued to inflict upon it.

Diamond Back Jones dragged his reins to his chest and shouted at the rest of the Indians through the clouds of swirling dust.

'Stop shooting, my brothers. Listen!'

The sound of the fleeing bounty hunter's mount filled all their ears as the Apache braves stopped their ponies next to the outlaw and their chief.

Slowly the dust drifted away from what remained of the painted warriors. The bodies of their less fortunate brothers soon became hideously evident on the blood-covered sand.

It was Conchowata who was first to spot their fleeing foe racing across the arid prairie atop the fresh mount. He raised his rifle and pointed at him through the dust.

'There!' Conchowata cried out. 'Iron Eyes has escaped!'

'Let's get him!' Diamond Back yelled out.

The Apache braves kicked the sides of their mounts and drove on after the dust of the bounty hunter.

Iron Eyes had managed to put a quarter of a mile between himself and the Apaches when he heard the screams starting once again behind him.

His eyes narrowed as he stared at the sandcoloured rocks before him. They were at least fifty feet high and seemed to go on for ever in both directions. As he drove the terrified pony towards the ridge, he began to see the cave half-way up more clearly.

Iron Eyes gritted his teeth and clung to the crude reins, a single strip of rope which was looped around the pony's head and through its open mouth.

'C'mon, horse!' the bounty hunter yelled at the small pinto. The terrified animal responded and increased its pace. Faster and faster the pony raced across the prairie until Iron Eyes began to realize that there was no safe trail through the high wall of sand-coloured rocks.

Looking over his shoulder, he could see that the Apaches were not going to quit. They wanted his scalp on a war lance. He looked up at the blazing sun and knew that there was less than an hour of daylight left before darkness came.

He spurred again.

Could he survive for another hour?

The thought haunted him. He had never before faced so many enemies at once. But it was not the sheer volume of Apache braves which troubled the bounty hunter, it was whether he had enough ammunition to hold them off until sunset.

The Apaches whom he had met in the past would not usually fight during the hours of darkness for fear of upsetting their gods. He wondered if these Apaches were the same. Would sunset bring him salvation?

Somehow, he doubted it.

When Iron Eyes reached the foot of

the ridge he pulled back on the rope and the mount's mane and stopped the terrified animal. He threw his right leg over its neck and slid on to the sand.

He glanced up at the cave and then back at the eighty or so Indians who were still baying for his blood. Gripping the saddle horn with his left hand, Iron Eyes steadied himself and tried to get his breath back. He watched the charging Apaches coming through the heat haze.

'Damn Apaches! Ain't they ever gonna quit?' He tried to spit but there was no moisture left in his entire body. For the first time he noticed the large half-full water bag hanging around the pony's neck. Iron Eyes used his knife to cut the rawhide strap and rested the bag on his broad bony left shoulder.

Its cool contents soothed his throat as his cold eyes darted between the approaching warriors and the high sandy ridge.

'Looks like I ain't got no place to go except up,' Iron Eyes drawled. 'This is turning out to be one real bad day.'

The sound of rifles being fired started again. The tall man snarled at the unholy vision which was heading through the swirling hot air towards him. He had managed to defy the odds so far but now there was nowhere left to ride.

Iron Eyes knew that the pinto was now useless. He pushed the pony away and watched as it ran off across the prairie. It had served its purpose and was now grateful to be away from the vicious spurs of the merciless bounty hunter.

Iron Eyes turned and looked at the ridge of solid rock that loomed over him. He knew that it would not be easy reaching the cave, but there was no alternative. It was either climb or die and Iron Eyes was not ready to die just yet.

If this was to be his last stand, he was going to try and take as many Apache with him as possible. He had no intention of going to hell on his own.

The tall figure ran to the foot of the rockface and started to climb.

5

Even trail dust could not disguise the fact that the elegant rider astride the black gelding was a man with whom it did not pay to toy. He looked every part a gunfighter and yet the marshal's star pinned to his silk vest told a very different story. This was an old-fashioned lawman, the sort that had mostly gone the way of the buffalo over the past couple of decades. Marshal Tom Quaid had been able to smell Dry Gulch more than an hour before his keen eyes had seen the whitewashed buildings shimmering in the heat haze.

He had steered his horse well since leaving Texas and never faltered in his relentless pursuit of the outlaw known as Diamond Back Jones. He knew that his star meant nothing here in the territories and he should have long since ended his chase, but Quaid was not a man to allow the mere limitations of the law prevent him from executing the warrant in his vest pocket.

Whatever it took, he was determined to get his man.

He wanted Diamond Back Jones either alive or dead. It made no difference, although there was a demon inside him that could think of nothing but killing the ruthless outlaw.

If it had been any other outlaw he would have observed the borders and admitted defeat. But this time it was different. This time it was personal.

For the first time since he had become a United States marshal, he had allowed his heart to overrule his fifty-three-year-old head. Ignored the twenty-eight years experience of upholding the law and allowed his fury to guide him.

This time he had hit the trail alone because he wanted no witnesses and no one along who might just point out when he overstepped the mark.

Quaid would be judge, jury and

executioner if need be. If he did break any of his precious laws, it would be he alone who would have to live with the consequences.

He had left Texas more than a month earlier and trailed the infamous outlaw further and further west until he realized that Diamond Back Jones was probably leading him into a trap. For he knew that this unforgiving landscape was home to the brutal Jones. Here the hunted would have the advantage. Yet Quaid did not worry over such things.

Tom Quaid was of the old school of lawmen. He lived by his gun skills because there had been a time when that had been the only way you could protect the innocent from the lawless vermin who roamed this big land.

It took a certain sort of man to live life on the knife-edge of almost daily danger. To face death and not be afraid. But Tom Quaid was that sort of man. A rare breed that never flinched away from trouble. A man who could never be bluffed.

For over a month the rider had thought about the reasons why he had set out on this quest. The haunting images had flashed through his mind in every waking moment and turned his sleep into nightmares. In nearly thirty years of being a lawman nothing had affected him this way before. There was only one reason why he was after the outlaw.

This was revenge. Pure and simple revenge. Diamond Back Jones would pay for what he had done back in Texas. Quaid had vowed that over the graves of his two daughters.

There was nowhere on the face of the earth that the veteran marshal would not go in order to catch the blood-thirsty killer. Even if it meant riding into the bowels of Hell itself. He would never stop his avenging pursuit.

If there had ever been any fear dwelling in the marshal, it had disappeared since that chilling moment when he had discovered the bodies of his only remaining family members on his ranch just outside Waco.

Their murders had somehow stripped every ounce of caution from Tom Quaid's soul. Now he had nothing left to lose except his life. But that was the one thing he had never truly valued.

Quaid pulled the front of his Stetson down until its brim was at eye-level. He knew that when facing his enemies it paid to be able to see their eyes without them being able to focus upon his. For the first to blink was usually also the first to die.

It had been a trick that had never let him down. He had managed to outdraw more than forty men in his long career and not lost a second's sleep over any of them.

For the vermin that tasted the lead of men like Tom Quaid were bad and death was their just reward for the pain they inflicted upon others. Lawmen like Quaid were the only upholders of justice available for the innocent in the West.

He pulled back on his reins and

slowed the tall black gelding as he entered the wide main street. He had heard tales of this town and its acrid aroma told him that every one of the stories must be true.

The sound of a million flies alerted the marshal that something other than stinking outhouses had excited them during the hot day. As he allowed his horse to pass the crude open-fronted funeral parlour, he realized what that something was. Blood-soaked bodies were stacked on top of one another. They spilled out on to the boardwalk. The sound of hammering echoed out from the rear of the building as coffins were being hastily assembled.

Tom Quaid inhaled through his gritted teeth and narrowed his eyes and continued on.

He knew that there had been a real big gun battle in Dry Gulch and wondered if Diamond Back Jones had anything to do with it.

There was no fear in Quaid. Others in his occupation might have hidden their gleaming star in a town such as Dry Gulch, but not him. He pushed the tails of his topcoat over the ivory grips of his Remingtons and allowed the star to catch the low red rays that indicated that the day was almost done. He aimed the head of his young horse towards the saloon and tapped his spurs gently to encourage it to reach the hitching rail.

His wrinkled eyes noticed the blood-stained sand and the walls that had been damaged by what could only have been a gun battle.

Quaid eased back in his saddle and stopped his mount. He sat looking all around at the nervous faces that peered at him from countless doorways and corners.

He dismounted and led the horse to a trough, then wrapped the reins around a pole. He stood defiant as his horse drank its fill.

'You lookin' for somebody, Marshal?' a large woman asked as she carried a bucket and mop along the boardwalk past the saloon front.

Quaid looked at her. He could see that this was one resident of Dry Gulch who actually worked honestly to make ends meet.

'Yep. I'm looking for a low-down critter named Diamond Back Jones, ma'am. You happen to know his whereabouts?'

She paused for a moment and pushed a long loose strand of hair off her face.

'Is he kinda dark?'

'Yep. He's a full-blood Apache.' Quaid nodded. 'Although he pretends to be white. A dangerous killer.'

Her face altered. It was obvious that she did not like Apaches.

'He's an Indian? Damn! I hate redskins and no mistake. He was in Dry Gulch 'til that bounty hunter came a-callin'. I figure that he got scared.'

'Bounty hunter?' The marshal stepped up on to the boardwalk and looked down into her face.

'Yeah. He was tall and mean and as thin as a beanpole,' she informed him.

'I never seen such a man before. His hair was long and kinda dirty. The word is that he wanted the bounty on Diamond Back. He sure got things all fired-up around here.'

'I've heard of a bounty hunter like that.' Quaid sighed, rubbing his chin. 'I think they call him Iron Eyes.'

She smiled broadly. 'That's his name OK. I heard the boys saying so. Iron Eyes. What kinda name is that? Is he an Indian too?'

'I don't think he is. What actually happened around here, ma'am?' Quaid inhaled again and stared into the low sun down the street towards the funeral parlour. 'I seen a stack of dead folks piled up down there.'

'There was one heck of a gunfight here earlier,' she said rolling her eyes. 'I thought that we was all gonna get killed the way them bullets was flying in all directions. Seems that Iron Eyes was after the same varmint as you.'

'Jones?'

'Yeah. Well, Jones paid some of the

local gutter rats to stop this Iron Eyes character whilst he made his getaway,' she said as she adjusted the mop in her hand.

Tom Quaid inhaled deeply through his nostrils. 'What happened?'

'That Iron Eyes killed the whole bunch of them and then lit out after Diamond Back again,' she gushed.

'He killed them all?' There was surprise in the veteran lawman's voice.

'Every darn one of them. Good riddance, I say. They were all scum like Jones himself.' She spat at the boardwalk as if demonstrating her disgust. 'They tried to bushwhack him and he didn't cotton to it.'

'Thank you, ma'am.' Quaid pulled out a silver dollar and offered it to the woman who gratefully accepted it and slid it into her ample cleavage.

'Thank you, Marshal,' she said. 'Say, I'd be careful if I was you. They don't cotton to the law in this darn town. There's still plenty of backshooters who'd kill ya for the gold in ya fillings.'

'In my experience, there ain't many towns which do cotton to the law, ma'am.' Tom Quaid smiled. 'And my teeth are storebought anyway.'

Quaid touched the brim of his Stetson and nodded. He watched as she went on her way.

'Who the hell are you, dude?'

The marshal turned to face the gravel voice that came from the saloon doorway. His eyes narrowed as he surveyed the large figure standing with one hand on the top of the swing-doors and the other resting on the grip of his Colt.

'You talking to me?' Quaid asked, squaring up to the man.

The dying rays of the sun flashed off the well polished star pinned to the silk vest.

'Are you a lawman, dude?' the man gruffed in a mixture of shock and surprise. 'Coz if'n ya are, ya must be damn loco to come to Dry Gulch.'

Quaid lowered his head slightly so that he could watch the eyes of his adversary.

'I'm looking for Diamond Back Jones, friend.'

The big man spat a lump of dark goo on to the bleached boards between them.

'He rode out hours back with that bounty hunter on his tail.'

'I know,' Quaid said, flexing his fingers over the grips of his guns.

'Then what are ya still doing in town?' the man growled like an angry bear. 'Get going. Your sort ain't welcome in Dry Gulch.'

'I figured that already, friend.' Quaid sighed heavily as he could sense that once more his gun skills would be tested. 'But if I was you, I'd go find myself a rock to hide behind.'

The man released his grip on the swing-doors and then lowered his hand to waist-level.

'We've had a real bad day here. I think ya ought to quit while you're ahead. Get going.'

'I'm going when I decide to go and not when some fat scum tells me. OK?'

the marshal said firmly.

'I ain't fat!' the man protested. 'I just got me big bones, ya old bastard.'

'Even your fingers are fat, son!' Tom Quaid said. 'You try to draw on me with those fingers and you'll surely regret it.'

The large man made a noise that sounded like a stuck pig. Whatever words might have spewed furiously from his mouth, the marshal could not understand any of them.

Quaid saw the man's right hand move as it began to haul the Colt from its holster. His own hands moved far more swiftly. Both his Remingtons were drawn from their hand-tooled holsters in one fraction of a heartbeat.

The marshal cocked the gun hammers and squeezed both triggers at exactly the same moment.

One bullet severed the holster from the large man's gunbelt as the other tore the battered Stetson off his head.

There was a look of astonishment on

the man's sweat-soaked face as his gun fell on to the boardwalk. His left hand patted the top of his head in a vain search for his hat.

'Stop fretting, tubby. Your head's still there,' Tom Quaid said. 'Not that you seem to use it much.'

'Who the hell are ya?' the confused figure asked.

'Tom Quaid.'

'I heard of ya. Texan trash.'

Quaid walked up to the large figure and poked one of his gun barrels into the bulging belly with as much force as he could muster. The man yelped. As the sweating head came forward it was met with the ivory gun grip which glanced across his chin-bone. The sound of teeth breaking echoed inside the large man's mouth. He staggered, then felt the boot catching him across his wide rear. The dazed man fell like a sack of potatoes on to the sand beside the boardwalk.

'Reckon you'll not try and draw on a stranger quite so quickly in future,'

Quaid said. The man rolled over on the sand until his bewildered face was looking straight at him. 'Some old folks are a damn sight more lively than they look.'

The marshal slid both his guns back into their holsters and shook his head in disbelief at the pitiful figure who was staring up at him.

'Tell me, my big-boned friend. What are you?'

'I'm an outlaw.' The man mumbled as blood and teeth fragments trickled from his mouth.

'An outlaw?' Quaid tried not to laugh.

'Yeah!' More blood fell from the crimson mouth. 'I'm an outlaw.'

Quaid exhaled. 'Well I suggest you quit, sonny. I reckon it's time you found yourself a new occupation.'

'What ya trying to say?'

Tom Quaid shouted down at the man. 'Find yourself a new career! You just ain't no good at this one, you dumb bastard.'

The large man watched helplessly as Quaid defiantly entered the saloon. Somehow, he knew that the veteran lawman was right.

6

The sky was on fire with every tone of red that nature could muster on its infinite palette, but the cornered bounty hunter had no time to notice. Bullets tore all around the mouth of the cave entrance as Iron Eyes lay on his belly with his long coat beside him. He had just managed to crawl into the cave only moments before the screaming Apache horsemen had reached the base of the ridge and started firing at him with their rifles and bows.

The arrows had no power in them by the time they had reached the high sanctuary but the bullets were as deadly as ever.

The Apaches continued firing for more than five minutes after they had witnessed their prey scrambling up the sand-coloured rocks and into the dark cave. Their bullets were relentless as they vainly tried to shoot the exhausted bounty hunter. Dust showered over Iron Eyes as he waited for the volley to ease up for just a single moment.

A heartbeat of precious time to try and work out what was happening to him.

All he needed was a little time to get his thoughts together so that he could work out what his next move should be.

If there was a next move.

Iron Eyes was beginning to wonder if this was how it was going to end. Was this his last stand? His personal Alamo?

Then suddenly the shooting eased up and eventually stopped.

Iron Eyes rose on to all fours and pushed his long dust-caked hair off his face. A sudden pain traced through his skull as he felt the bloody graze on his scalp with his thin fingers.

He stared at his hand and the blood which covered it.

Iron Eyes knew that he was bleeding again but that was nothing new for the gaunt man. He had lost more blood over the years than probably now flowed through his veins, because of the wounds his enemies had inflicted upon him.

He rubbed the blood on to his torn and tattered shirt and sighed heavily.

Iron Eyes leaned over the edge of the high rocks and fired his guns at the figures far below him. Even in the haunting red light of the setting sun, he could still see them. He watched with no emotion as another handful of the more determined Indians were hit by his deadly accuracy.

Their lifeless bodies crashed down over the jagged rocks.

Iron Eyes studied the remainder of the tribe taking cover far below the cave. He had spotted Diamond Back Jones in his outlaw clothing moving with the rest of the heavily armed braves behind the rocks and sparse brush. But they were out of range of his Navy Colts.

'Damn you, Diamond Back!' he cursed angrily as he thought about the bounty on the outlaw's head. Dead or alive, $1,000. It was a reward that might never be collected the way things were going.

More bullets hit the roof of the cave above him as the Apache retaliated to his killing even more of their number. But this time Iron Eyes did not flinch as red-hot tapers of lethal lead passed within inches of him.

Blood trickled down the limp strands of hair that hung in front of his narrowed eyes. He could feel his scalp throbbing as the graze continued to bleed.

The bounty hunter knew that this was not his sort of fight and that the Indians had the advantage. They had rifles which had far greater range than his pistols. Iron Eyes was used to fighting men up close. He liked to see the whites of his enemies' eyes before he killed them.

With the fading light, he was now even more vulnerable. They were calling the shots and all he could do was take everything they dished out and try to survive.

Iron Eyes did not like it.

He was the hunter! Not them!

How could he have gotten himself into this situation? His head ached as it tried to work out what exactly had happened to turn the tables on him.

But no matter how much he tried, he could not work it out.

Iron Eyes piled every bullet he could find in the long coat's deep pockets beside him and carefully reloaded the Navy Colts. He had roughly eighty rounds left from the two boxes he had emptied out on the prairie.

It seemed that there were probably as many if not more Apache left below him.

Iron Eyes was slowly beginning to realize that he could no longer afford to miss. He had lost that luxury. Every single bullet had to count or he would be reduced to trying to fend them off with the Bowie knife in his boot.

Did he have enough rounds to get them all?

74

The thought haunted him.

The sun was sinking lower and lower and yet every minute seemed like an eternity. As more rifle bullets continued to splinter off the soft golden rock surface around him, he wondered what would happen when all his bullets were gone.

He had always been the hunter.

Now it was he who was trapped like one of the animals or outlaws he had chased over the years.

Iron Eyes did not like the feeling because he knew that it was always the hunter who had the advantage. The hunter knew when he was going to strike. How he was going to outwit his prey.

Iron Eyes removed the crude stopper from the Indian water bag and lifted it to his cracked lips. He swallowed the still-cool liquid, then sighed heavily.

His attention was drawn into the cave. It seemed to stretch off into the distance but he could not be sure of anything in the darkness.

'The way my luck's been goin' today, I reckon that there must be a bear or puma in them shadows,' Iron Eyes mumbled to himself as more shots rang out from below him.

A million pieces of rock showered over him again as the rifle bullets hit the roof of the cave directly above his head.

Iron Eyes flinched again as the small stones cascaded on to his bleeding scalp.

'No wonder I hate Apaches!' he spat.

Yet no matter how angry he found himself becoming, he knew he had to remain calm. He could not afford to waste any of his bullets with so many men seeking to kill him.

He placed one of his guns beside the bullets and cocked the hammer of the other, then edged his way back to the lip of the cave. He squinted down and aimed carefully at the braves who were ascending the rocks.

He squeezed the trigger.

The deafening noise bounced off the damp walls that surrounded him, but he did not notice. His entire attention was on his chosen target.

Another of the Indians was dead. He repeated the action again and again until the warriors were either dead or had retreated out of range of his Navy Colt.

He moved back into the relative safety of the cave and tried to think. It was almost impossible as his head pounded like a million war drums. He knew that he ought to have a plan by now, but there was nothing in his mind except the instinct to survive.

Iron Eyes dragged his coat towards him, reached into the inside pocket and pulled out a handful of cigars. They were all broken but could still be smoked.

His eyes drifted up and looked at the sun again. It was now sinking beneath the distant horizon.

He struck a match with his thumb-nail and touched the end of the cigar between his teeth. Smouldering leaf fell on to his legs as he puffed on the putrid smoke.

Would these Apaches stop once the sun had set?

He opened the gun's chamber and allowed the hot casings to fall on to the cave floor as he plucked another six bullets off the pile beside him.

One by one he slid the bullets into the narrow holes before closing the chamber again and locking it. He cocked the hammer and sucked hard on the cigar as the sun finally disappeared.

Darkness seemed to sweep over him like a blanket.

7

Marshal Tom Quaid had wasted no time in riding out after the outlaw Diamond Back Jones and the bounty hunter who already seemed to have managed to kill more men in one day than his notorious prey had done in the previous few years. Quaid had purchased a fresh mount in the sunbleached town and driven the chestnut mare far harder than he had ever driven any horse before. Quaid had tied the bridle of his black gelding to his saddle cantle and led the horse across the arid prairie until his fresh mount was totally exhausted.

Only when Tom Quaid was convinced that his new mount could no longer maintain the speed he had demanded of it, did he dismount and transfer his saddle and trail bags to the black gelding. He left the lathered-up chestnut and rode on.

The black gelding had managed to keep pace with the chestnut mare easily, having no saddle or trail tack on its back. Now it was also being forced to race across the hard ground beneath the bright moon as its master tried to gain on the two men who were ahead of him. The marshal knew that using two mounts instead of one had enabled him to reduce the distance between them by several hours.

It was not the first time he had used this trick to gain on his prey. But there had never been so much urgency in his desire to catch up with anyone before.

He wanted Diamond Back Jones.

There was nothing that could stop him.

After more than two hours of forcing the long-legged gelding to continue its reckless pace, Quaid eventually drew in his reins, stood in his stirrups and gazed ahead across the moonlit prairie. He had managed to get all the information concerning Diamond Back Jones that he required back at Dry Gulch. Even the town's most drunken of men realized that the veteran lawman was more than capable of using the matched Remington pistols he sported.

They had told him everything that he had wanted to know about the elusive outlaw and the strange bounty hunter who was chasing him.

But there had been no mention that the trail both riders had taken led deep into Apache territory. It seemed to the lawman that the citizens of Dry Gulch had conveniently forgotten that small detail.

Marshal Quaid dismounted from the tired mount. He removed one of the four canteens from the saddle horn and then slowly unscrewed its stopper.

The sound of gunfire out in the distance had led him to this place. But with the setting of the merciless sun, the shooting had suddenly stopped. Quaid knew that meant that the men firing their rifles had to be Indians. Most probably one of the numerous Apache tribes which reigned supreme in this desolate land.

He dropped his Stetson on to the ground before the black gelding and poured half the canteen's contents into the upturned hat. He then sipped at the water, never once taking his eyes off the distant rocky ridges which were now illuminated by the bright moon.

Quaid knew that the shooting had come from somewhere directly ahead of him. He had aimed his mount straight at the sound of the shooting until it had ceased more than an hour earlier. He glanced down at the ground and could still see the two sets of hoof tracks less than a few feet away from his mount. Even in the moonlight, the trail was clear.

His eyes drifted back up to the distant ridge. It was deathly silent out there now but Quaid knew that meant nothing.

Every instinct told him that he was now venturing into unknown territory. He had never had any dealings with Indians during his long career as a law officer but he knew that there was no alternative for him.

He had to keep following the trail.

He wanted Jones.

Jones was an Apache.

To get him, he had to continue onwards.

The water tasted bitter to the dry-mouthed marshal but he carried on drinking until his thirst was quenched. He returned the stopper to the neck of the canteen and secured it before hanging it back on the saddle horn.

The sound of many rifles had rung out across the arid land earlier. So many rifles that Quaid began to wonder exactly how many Apaches there were out there. Twenty? Fifty? A hundred or more?

Even a half-dozen of them would be more than most men could cope with. A cold shiver traced down his spine.

A million thoughts crept through his mind. Who were the Apache firing at? Was Iron Eyes their target? If so, how was it that the shooting had carried on for so long?

It seemed strange to the lawman that any one man could maintain a battle with so many Indians for such a long time.

Who was this Iron Eyes character anyway?

Whoever he was, he seemed to have a knack of surviving against all odds.

Quaid removed his bandanna from his neck and wiped the mixture of sweat and dust from his face. He was troubled by the way things were going.

Vengeance had driven him for so long that he had become almost impervious to anything else except the man he wanted to capture and kill. Quaid knew that he had allowed the green-eyed demon of hatred to drive him into a situation that he was ill-equipped to handle.

Now it was no longer the hunter and the hunted.

Now the Apache nation was in the stewpot.

Diamond Back Jones had managed to stay ahead of his pursuers long enough to return to his people. Tom Quaid knew that his marshal's star meant even less to Indians than it had to the people back in Dry Gulch.

This was not going to be easy.

He had faced gangs of killers before but never a whole tribe of angry Indians. And Apaches were more ruthless than most of their brothers further north.

How did you fight the Apache?

It had sounded as if the bounty hunter was doing a good job of it before sunset. Maybe the darkness held the key, Quaid thought.

The marshal lifted his hat off the ground and shook it before carefully returning it to his white-haired head. He inhaled, grabbed hold of the saddle horn and mounted.

To have any chance of getting Jones away from his fellow Apaches, the marshal wondered if he ought to try and reach them before dawn.

If there was a single chance of capturing the man who had murdered his daughters, it was during the hours of darkness. Yet the brilliant moon was almost as bright as the noonday sun.

Quaid felt another shiver trace his spine.

He had heard tales that the Apache would not fight during the night. The shooting had certainly stopped as soon as the sun had set, but perhaps there had been another reason for that.

Quaid rubbed his jawline.

Perhaps the reason for the end of the shooting was that the Apache had finally managed to kill the bounty hunter known as Iron Eyes.

Could that be it?

Had the Apache only stopped fighting because they had already destroyed their enemy? Would they turn their rifles upon him once he turned up?

He swallowed hard and tapped his spurs again.

The black gelding started to canter as its master continued to brood.

Tom Quaid still had a million questions filling his mind as his mount gathered pace. The trouble was, he now had a million answers too.

Which one was right?

He knew that he would find out when he reached the high moonlit ridge. Until then, he could do nothing except ride.

8

Iron Eyes had watched the moon move
across the heavens and knew that it
must be more than an hour since the
Apache had stopped attacking him.
They were still down there amid the
brush and rocks. He could smell the
food they were cooking even though he
could not make out where their
camp-fire was. Yet Iron Eyes was
seldom hungry at the best of times, and
this was far from being the best of
times. Only one thought filled his mind
as droplets of blood continued to drip
from the limp strands of his long hair:
was it possible to escape? Nothing had
ever defeated him before, but this time
he knew that he was in a pretty tight
spot. Since the Apache had stopped
their attack he had used up the
seemingly eternal time to good purpose. He had used the razor-sharp edge

of his knife to trim all the cigar fragments he had found in his pockets into a score of smaller smokes.

And he had waited.

Waited to see if the Indians were trying to fool him into thinking that they would not fight during the night. So far they had not tried to do anything and the bounty hunter began to believe that he was safe until sunrise. He gripped one of the cigar trimmings in his teeth and looked around the cave as the moonlight crept deeper into it. The cave was like a tomb. A burial place waiting for a corpse to fill its large belly. Iron Eyes had no intention of being that corpse.

When the sun had set he had wondered if it were possible for him to climb down from the high cave, steal one of the Apache ponies and make his escape. It had been a idea which had soon evaporated when the large bright moon had risen over the prairie to replace the blazing sun.

The moon was big and bright and

there wasn't a cloud in the sky that might give him cover.

Iron Eyes knew there was no escape using the same route that had brought him to this high vantage point. The haunting blue moonlight ensured that he remained inside the cave.

The Indians had been strangely silent since darkness had swept over the ridge and prairie. Yet they were still down there amid the brush and rocks. Now though he could hear the chilling sound of their chanting voices drifting on the warm night air.

Iron Eyes knew that they were singing to their gods.

Like the bounty hunter, they were still wide awake.

Awake and watching the mouth of the cave.

But unlike the Apache, Iron Eyes had no gods to turn to and pray to for help. He was alone, as he had always been. Alone with only his own demons for company.

Iron Eyes knew that there were no

more than seven hours of darkness at this time of the year and at least one of them had already come and gone.

He rose to his feet and felt the roof of the cave touch his tender scalp. He stooped and moved deeper into the cave trying to work out how far it went into the ridge.

Could this be a tunnel which actually went right the way through the sand-coloured rock?

Iron Eyes found his matches again, struck one on the cave wall and stared deeper into the dark natural tunnel. It seemed to go on for quite a long way. The match went out when its flame seemed to catch a small draught.

The bounty hunter was curious.

He ignited another match with his thumbnail and held it ahead of him toward the back of cave.

Again the flame was blown out.

Iron Eyes knew that there was a gentle breeze blowing through the cave from somewhere far into the ridge of sandy stone. Was there a way out of here?

There had to be, he surmised. Fresh air did not come out of the bowels of the earth. But it did flow through tunnels.

The tall man returned to his coat and guns. He scooped the coat off the ground and put it on before picking up his prized Navy Colts and tucking them into his belt. He knelt and picked up every one of the bullets and dropped them into his deep pockets, then he placed the Apache water bag on his left shoulder.

Placing another of his small trimmed cigars between his teeth, Iron Eyes started to walk carefully towards the rear of the cave with his arms outstretched. He knew that he needed a torch to guide him but the cave had nothing in it but dust.

Sweat and blood ran down his face and dripped from the jaw of the tall man as he felt his way further and further into the blackness.

It was so dark that Iron Eyes felt as if he were totally blind. Without sight, he had to rely upon his other senses to guide him.

There seemed to be no reason for it but the walls of the cave seemed to be getting warmer the deeper he went into the black tunnel. Maybe the rocks had absorbed every ounce of the blazing sun's heat during the day and it was only after sunset that the sand-coloured stone was able to release it, he thought.

With every step of his long legs Iron Eyes knew that he was probably venturing into a place where no other living man had ever gone before. The rocks felt warmer as his hands groped along their rough surfaces. He could hear water dripping far ahead of him and smell the scent of air as it traced past his flared nostrils. Even his scarred skin could sense the touch of a gentle breeze.

Iron Eyes wondered why this should be. If there was a way out of this cave somewhere down the tunnel, why was there no light to be seen?

Again he caught the scent of fresh prairie air mixed with the warm stale cave air which surrounded him.

Somewhere there was an opening that was allowing air to flow through the cave tunnel.

He had to keep going until he found that opening. Iron Eyes hoped that when he eventually reached it, it would be big enough for him to squeeze through and escape.

The tunnel seemed to drop away from him. Carefully, the bounty hunter felt his way down a steep incline. Then the cave floor appeared to level out again. He continued groping his way slowly along the black passage of stone. Again the ground beneath his mule-ear boots fell away and he had to cling to either side of the cave walls just to maintain his balance. Iron Eyes slid for more than ten feet on his side until his boots felt the ground beneath them once more. He stood and began walking again.

No wonder he could not see the other cave mouth, he thought. It must be on a far lower level.

The cool breeze was stronger now and grew even stronger with every step that he took. Iron Eyes adjusted the water bag on his shoulder and realized that there was now far more head room above him. He carried on making his way along the black tunnel until once more he sensed that he was moving down another steep incline.

Step after step he managed to find his way down to the next level part of the cave floor. He stopped and rested for a few moments and lowered the water bag from his shoulder. He pulled its stopper and drank. The cold water refreshed him enough to make him aware that there was something in the tunnel.

Suddenly, a chilling sound filled his ears.

A sound that he recognized.

Iron Eyes lowered the water bag and dropped it next to his left leg as he listened. His eyes tried desperately to see but it was just too dark. Even his keen eyes could not locate the thing that had frozen him to the spot.

Again the sound echoed around the cave walls.

There was no mistaking it.

The rattle began to grow louder.

'Rattler!' he whispered under his breath. He had lost count of how many times he had bumped into the strange unpredictable creatures in the past. But this was the first time that he had been unable to see the deadly viper who warned its prey with the rattle at the end of its vibrating tail.

Iron Eyes lowered his right arm from off the rough wall surface and moved it slowly towards the pistol grips that poked out from his belt.

His long bony fingers wrapped around one of the handles of his matched Navy Colts and began to pull it free of his belt. As its barrel cleared the belt, the sound grew even louder.

The sound of the sidewinder's rattle

was now furious.

Iron Eyes cocked the gun hammer until it fully locked, then he desperately used his ears to try and locate the poisonous snake. He thought about the matches in his shirt pocket. If he were to ignite one, he might be able to see his target. But he knew that a rattler could strike out far faster than it would take his own eyes to adjust.

Sweat dripped from his face as if someone had poured a canteen of water over his head. Iron Eyes knew that the snake was ready to strike. It had to be coiled if its rattle was making so much noise. A moving sidewinder was usually silent.

The barrel of his gun swayed back and forth as he blindly searched for the deadly viper.

With only the noisy tail of the snake to guide him, Iron Eyes had to try and work out where its head might be. All he could tell for certain was that the snake was close.

Too close.

97

He gritted his teeth and bit through the unlit cigar. He knew that he had to try and kill this creature with his first shot, for once the bullet left the barrel the blinding light would most probably make the rattler strike.

Angry snakes always struck out at their enemies.

Iron Eyes tried to ignore the sound of his pounding heart as it beat frantically inside his painfully thin frame. He concentrated on the sound of the rattler and tried to aim the gun at it.

He inhaled deeply. Held his breath and fired.

The white explosion of light blinded the bounty hunter and the sound as the firing pin hit the bullet was deafening.

Frantically Iron Eyes cocked the hammer again and listened hard for the snake's rattle. He could hear nothing above the ringing in his ears. Wherever the sidewinder was, he was going to taste more lead, the bounty hunter thought.

He fired again and again in a

desperate bid to kill the unseen snake.

When the ringing in his ears eventually stopped, Iron Eyes strained to hear the sound of the tail. There was nothing but silence.

Sweat and blood continued to seep from his scalp into the darkness as he licked his dry lips in a vain attempt to rid his mouth of the bitter taste of gunsmoke.

Had he succeeded in killing the snake?

It was possible considering that he had tried to group his bullets tightly in the general direction that he thought the sound of the sidewinder's tail had come from.

But had he hit it?

Perhaps he had only frightened it away to lie in wait for him further into the black cave tunnel! The thought troubled the tall crouching figure.

He inhaled deeply and decided that nothing would be gained by remaining here. He had to carry on and try and find out where the gentle draught of cool night air was coming from.

Iron Eyes bent his knees and groped for the water bag's neck until he located it beside his leg. He slowly straightened, up and placed the cool bag over his broad left shoulder.

He must have hit it, he thought. Even without the sense of sight, he had killed too many things to suddenly lose the honed knack of bringing death to his chosen prey.

The gentle breeze hit his face again and made him look straight ahead into the impenetrable darkness. It was stronger now and he could smell the scent of sagebrush. He was close to his goal.

Cautiously he moved his right leg forward to continue his search for the elusive cave mouth exit. It had only gone a matter of inches when he felt something hit the side of his boot. The snake's powerful fangs penetrated his boot and sank deeply into his flesh.

He staggered and fell heavily. He felt the water bag fall off his shoulder as he twisted on the sand in the blackness. Pain tore through him. He kicked out his legs but knew that the rattler's fangs were still buried into his calf muscle, the creature unwilling or unable to release its hold on him.

It felt as though a million poisonous needles were racing through his body at exactly the same moment. He rolled over and over trying to escape the unseen enemy who was forcing its fangs deeper into his flesh.

His entire body crashed into the cave wall. For a brief moment he felt flames burning inside his guts. It was as if his very soul was being consumed by an inferno of poison. He scrambled back on to his feet and then grabbed at his skull as it filled with a legion of bursting colours.

With venom pumping into his leg, Iron Eyes screamed out in agony.

9

The sounds of bullets had alerted the Apache that something was happening in the high cave, but it was the blood-chilling scream which had echoed out of the cave mouth high on the moonlit ridge that drew every Indian's eyes in a mixture of shock and fear.

It had sounded like something from another world to the painted braves. None of them could believe that anything on this earth was capable of making such a horrific sound.

None of the tribe had ever heard anything like the noise which had bellowed out above them. The painted braves ran in confusion and gathered around the silent figure of their chief, Conchowata.

'What was that?' It was as if every one of the braves asked exactly the same question at the very same moment. The chief glanced at Diamond Back Jones who was sitting on his saddle next to his grazing horse.

'Has my brother ever heard such a sound in his time with the white eyes?' Conchowata asked.

Diamond Back Jones rose from his saddle near the blazing camp-fire and strode across the sand until he could see the high cave.

'Even a stuck pig don't make that kinda noise, chief.'

'Then what was it?' Conchowata asked the outlaw.

'I have never heard anything like that, great chief,' Jones admitted as he felt a bead of sweat run down from his hairline and drip from his furrowed brow. 'But we know that the evil one is up there. Could he have killed something in the cave, or maybe it killed him?'

'Nothing of this earth made that noise,' one of the Apache warriors said.

'The shooting was real enough though!' Jones muttered as he tried to work out if it were possible for the bounty hunter to have cried out so chillingly.

'The evil one tried to kill something up there!' a warrior suggested.

'Was it a demon?' Conchowata swallowed hard as the question came from his lips. 'Could there be a demon in that cave?'

'I don't know,' Jones admitted. He stepped even closer to the ridge and continued to stare up at the small cave opening far above them.

'Could a man make such a noise?' another of the warriors asked.

Diamond Back Jones rubbed his face. 'I have heard many men cry out in pain and fear, but none of them sounded like that.'

Conchowata rested a hand on the shoulder of the Apache who was dressed like a white man. Jones's head turned and looked into his chief's eyes.

'Do you think that there are animals up there in the cave, my brother? One of which was killed by the bullets of the evil one?'

'Or killed the one called Iron Eyes!' another brave said.

Jones returned his eyes to the cave. The light of the moon made the entire ridge appear to be glowing in an unholy shade of blue.

'What animal could reach that place? The cave is too far up for most animals to reach.'

'A mountain lion could!' another of the braves declared firmly. 'They can leap ten times their own height. A lion could reach the cave in three or four strides.'

Jones nodded.

'That is true. But was it an animal that cried out or Iron Eyes?'

'But was that the sound of a lion?' the chief asked, feeling the hairs on the nape of his neck tingle in fear beneath his long grey hair.

'I think not!' Jones shrugged.

'Are there evil spirits in that place?' the eldest son of the chief asked.

Conchowata had seen many things in his long life and knew that a wise chief never dismissed anything. For as soon as a man said that something did not exist, it usually appeared and made him look foolish.

'I can not say, Geroma. But whatever made that sound, it was either to mark injury or death.'

Diamond Back Jones sighed heavily, pulled his guns from their holsters and checked their chambers.

'I'm going up there, Conchowata.'

The sound of disbelief raced through the assembled Indians as they watched Jones start to walk towards the foot of the rugged rockface.

'Do not go up there, my brother!' Conchowata demanded as he paced after the Apache outlaw. 'The gods will not allow any of our people to fight after the sun has set. You know that is bad medicine.'

Diamond Back Jones looked again into the familiar eyes of the chief.

'I have lived with the white eyes long

enough to know that there is no such thing as bad medicine, Conchowata. Only bullets make medicine. I have killed many white eyes since leaving the tribe. Many of them during the hours of night. I am not afraid. I'm going up there to see if Iron Eyes is still there.'

The chief grabbed Jones's arm firmly.

'I am chief! I say no!'

'This is nonsense! I wanna see if the evil Iron Eyes is still alive up there! For all we know it was he who screamed out. Maybe there is an animal up there and it has killed him!'

'What if he is still alive?' Geroma asked as he stood next to his father.

Jones narrowed his eyes.

'If he is alive, I shall kill him, Geroma!'

'You cannot defy the gods!' Conchowata raged. 'This is our land but we are only here because of the mercy of our gods. We cannot fight until the sun rises.'

Diamond Back Jones pulled his arm free of the chief's grip and waved his hands at the rest of the tribe.

'No wonder our people have been driven into such arid lands by the white eyes. You are all women who fear unseen gods and allow our enemies to take advantage of us.'

Conchowata squared up to the outlaw.

'You will not go up there to fight!'

'I can and I will!' Diamond Back retorted.

Conchowata signalled to his braves. They all advanced with their daggers drawn.

The two men gazed angrily into each other's souls. Neither was willing to back down.

10

For more than five eternal minutes the bounty hunter had been racked by feverish delirium as he rolled over and over on the floor of the cave tunnel. His mind was melting into a soup of confused fog, yet he was fighting the unseen enemy which surged through his veins and arteries with every scrap of his dogged determination. Iron Eyes gritted his teeth as his entire body arched in violent agony for the umpteenth time.

He had suffered many things since he first stood upright and challenged the world, but nothing that came close to the pain he was now consumed by. Pain was one thing but to lose control of your mind made him angry.

He had always been a fighter and would never allow anything to defeat him without giving of his best. He had to try and beat this too. Whatever was happening to him as the poison infested his body, he would try and fight it.

Sweat had soaked his long hair as he had tried to escape the monsters who now brought nightmares to his fevered brain. It clung to his wet face like spiders' webs. He punched out violently at the black air trying to hit the invisible foes who tormented him. His knuckles glanced across the cave walls taking the skin off them but he did not feel a thing except the cruel venom which continued to tear through his innards.

The bounty hunter threw himself through the blackness at the wall of the cave as if attempting to knock himself out. Anything to escape the vicious torment which was engulfing him.

Sweat poured from him as the snake's venom flowed through his bloodstream. He felt as if his head were about to explode when he managed to regain part of his wits.

Without even knowing why, he grabbed the handle of the long Bowie knife protruding from the tall neck of his boot and hauled it out. He shook his head in a vain attempt to free his mind from the fog and thunder which was overwhelming him. Again he managed to regain his thoughts for the briefest of seconds and honed his every thought on the rattler which still clung to his leg.

The snake's fangs had driven so deeply into his boot and calf-muscle that it could no longer free itself.

Iron Eyes shook the sweat off his face and then groped for the viper's neck in the darkness. He found the wriggling serpent and squeezed it as hard as he could as the snake's body wrapped around his arm.

With the other hand Iron Eyes moved the long honed blade closer to the sidewinder. Pain racked his head and body as if he were being torn apart by a hundred wild mustangs but he continued to force himself to try and kill the creature that had almost certainly killed him.

His heart pounded in his chest as it tried to fight the poison which was now being sucked through his heart. Iron Eyes felt giddy and rolled over. His skull hit the cave wall. It was like a slap in the face for the feverish man. Suddenly he remembered what he was doing and tightened his grip on the snake's neck once more. The lethal blade of his knife sought out the neck of the rattler in the darkness. He could feel it cut his hand time and time again as he searched for the head of the snake. The hand holding the rattler became wet with his blood, but he could not feel the injuries he was inflicting upon himself.

They were mere scratches compared to the agony which racked the rest of him.

The snake's venom had deadened his entire body to anything except itself. Then the bounty hunter slid the curved blade under his thumb and pressed it into the throat of the determined sidewinder.

'Gotcha, ya bastard!' Iron Eyes growled.

He dragged the knife across the flesh of the snake with every ounce of his remaining strength. The body was severed from the head of the rattler but its fangs were still buried deep into his calf muscle. The poison still pumped from the twin fangs even though the creature was now dead.

Iron Eyes felt himself fall on to his side again. He was tired and yet knew that he dare not allow himself to sleep. For sleep meant certain death.

A swirling sickness seemed to be flowing into his mind. He could hear his heart beating like a drum. Louder and louder until he thought that he would go insane.

'No!' He cried out angrily forcing himself back up into a sitting position. 'No damn snake's gonna get the better of me. I ain't ready to go under just yet!'

Iron Eyes released his grip on the body of the snake and then poked the long edge of his Bowie knife into his boot. He dragged its razor sharp edge through the leather until it reached the fangs of the rattler still embedded in his leg.

He searched with the fingers of his free hand until he located the fangs, then placed the blade of his knife beneath them.

As if he were sawing wood, Iron Eyes carved at the creature until he felt it finally prised free from his flesh. He threw the head across the cave tunnel and began to feel as if he were about to pass out. He knew that if he did, he would never awaken again.

Iron Eyes inhaled deeply and tried to recall what he had planned to do next. He reached down and dragged the split boot off his foot and then pulled his leg up across his lap. He wiped his fingers free of the blood and blindly searched for the wounds left by the snake's fangs.

He could feel the blood and venom weeping under his fingers.

'Gotta do somethin'!' Iron Eyes

mumbled as his head filled with agonizing bolts of lightning. 'But what? Think, dammit! Think!'

Suddenly the bounty hunter remembered the matches in his shirt pocket. He rested the knife on his bleeding leg and shook his coat off his shoulders. Without even knowing why, he removed the box of matches from his pocket and then tore his shirt from his back.

Another sickening feeling overwhelmed him. His head rolled and fell against the cave wall beside him. He heard his skull crack under the impact but he felt no pain.

He started to count.

Louder and louder until he recalled what he was doing.

Somehow Iron Eyes forced himself back up on to his rear. His hands found the shirt again and he placed it next to his leg. He fumbled with the matches until he located one and struck it across the hard stone wall beside him.

The flame was almost blinding when it first ignited but within seconds its flame calmed down. Iron Eyes placed the match to his shirt and watched it catch alight. He pulled out a crumpled wanted poster from his deep coat pocket and placed it on the small blaze.

His bony fingers managed to pick up one of his bullets from out of the same pocket. Iron Eyes placed it between his small sharp teeth and then bit it with all his might. He felt the casing bend slightly. The acrid taste of gunpowder granules found the tip of his tongue before his fingers carefully removed the damaged bullet. Iron Eyes picked up his knife and prised the small lead ball from the bullet casing. He discarded the ball and put the casing next to his bleeding leg.

Iron Eyes blinked several times before he managed to focus upon the two weeping fang marks.

Without a second thought, he stabbed the leg with the point of the Bowie knife and watched as blood spurted out from the gash. He slid the blade across his calf from one fang hole to the next and then started to rip at the wound until he was satisfied that blood was pouring from it.

How much poison would also flow from his leg, he wondered.

His eyes suddenly went foggy. He stopped and shook his head until his mind began to clear once more. When he managed to focus on the wound again, Iron Eyes dropped his knife and squeezed both sides of his leg hard. More blood gushed out of the nasty knife wound. He could feel his chest tightening as the poison raced through him.

'C'mon! Get this done!' Iron Eyes snarled at himself.

He picked up the bullet casing and then poured the gunpowder into the deep gash. He felt the black granules burn like branding irons but ignored it. This pain was nothing compared to the agonizing turmoil the dead rattler's venom was still inflicting.

Iron Eyes plucked a burning fragment of his shirt and dropped it on to the gunpowder-laced wound.

A white flash exploded and knocked the bounty hunter flat on to his back. He lay there for several minutes staring at the flickering light on the roof of the cave tunnel.

The smell of burning flesh filled his nostrils after a few moments and forced him back up until he was seated again. He fumbled in his coat pockets and found another wanted poster and dropped that on to the small fire at his side.

His eyes rolled in his head until they found the gruesome sight of his charred calf muscle. The blackened flesh was no longer bleeding.

Iron Eyes picked up the body of the snake and shook it. The rattle still worked. He cut it free from the body and pushed it into his deep coat pocket.

Even half-dead, the hunter in his Iron Eyes soul still wanted a trophy of his kill.

'Gotta get out of here,' he told himself firmly. He rolled on to his knees and tried to regain his thoughts amid the toxic confusion that still tore through his head and every sinew. He clawed at the cave wall and got to his feet.

He was upright for the first time in what felt like an eternity and intended to remain that way. He knew that now he had to walk out of this unholy place. If death wanted him, it would have to claim him on his feet.

Every movement seemed to feel like a thousand knives being thrust into his thin pitiful frame. He used the last of the fire's light to pluck his long trail coat off the blood-soaked ground. After putting it back on, he gathered up his knife and guns and dropped them into his deep trail coat pockets. He slid his foot into what was left of his right boot and then scooped the water bag up and began to stagger down the sloping cave tunnel.

He continued on his journey.

But this time he was using the cave walls to support him as he fought with the demons that were filling his thoughts.

The fire finally went out behind him.

The half-dead Iron Eyes was walking in total darkness again.

He did not notice.

11

Matty Hume, Col Wall and Tanny
Gibson had been Texas Rangers for
more than twenty years between them.
Yet the current mission that they had
been sent on had nothing to do with
Texas, or any other civilized place for
that matter. Captain Matty Hume had
been given the unenviable job of trying
to trace the whereabouts of Marshal
Tom Quaid.

It seemed that the marshal had
friends in high places who knew that
the grieving lawman was hell bent on
finding the notorious outlaw known
only as Diamond Back Jones. It seemed
that there were powerful people who
had political plans for the veteran law
officer Tom Quaid. To them he was a
man who could bridge the gap between
the old and the new Texas.

The last thing the politicians wanted

was for those ambitions to be scuppered by Quaid himself breaking the very laws that he had spent a lifetime upholding.

Tom Quaid could simply not be allowed to administer his own form of justice. Yet the three riders knew that they would probably be driven by the same feelings of revenge if someone had brutally murdered their daughters.

Matty Hume had been given one simple order. He had to try and find Quaid before Quaid found Diamond Back Jones. Find the lawman and bring him back to Waco.

It was not a job the seasoned Texas Ranger had wanted but he knew that there were few others in his platoon who could match his own tracking skills. He had also never been a man to refuse any request from his superiors simply because there was an element of danger attached to it.

Hume had known Quaid for more than a decade and grown to admire the silver-haired marshal. The Texas Ranger knew that this was out of character for the lawman, but he understood it.

He also knew that Tom Quaid would never forgive himself if he did kill the outlaw in cold blood.

Captain Hume had asked for volunteers in the Texas Ranger outpost just west of Waco, but only two men had responded to the lean man's request for help.

Col Wall was roughly five feet nine inches in height with light-brown-coloured hair. His face was broad and looked as though it had taken a lot of punches over its thirty years but the green eyes sparkled with the joy of just being what he was. He was a Texas Ranger and no man could ever have equalled his pride in that simple fact.

Tanny Gibson was the least capable of the trio. Yet he had worked hard to try and make himself worthy of the badge he had been given thirteen months earlier. Gibson wanted to be as good as the two riders he rode with. Few other Rangers could equal his ambition and commitment.

Rangers Wall and Gibson were always willing to follow their captain. They knew that he was one Texas Ranger officer who never took risks with the lives of those in his company and always led from the front. Matty Hume was no armchair general like so many others of his rank. He would never ask his men to go anywhere he was unwilling to go himself.

That one simple fact gave his men confidence and trust, two key factors when you were riding into uncharted terrain.

The three riders had trailed Tom Quaid across the high border mountains and then down into the devilishly hot prairie that led into the unmapped and unnamed territory west of the sprawling Lone Star State.

Captain Matty Hume had few equals when it came to following trails and had led his two followers across more than a hundred miles of the most diverse land to be found anywhere in the vast continent.

The three horsemen had visited Dry Gulch and managed to leave its boundaries unscathed. They had purchased enough provisions and water in the stinking town to last them at least two weeks for they had no idea of how big the arid prairie that stretched out before them was.

Even the hours of night could not slow their pace.

Hume stood in his stirrups and took the weight off his mount's shoulders. His sharp eyesight studied the moonlit hoof-tracks that led off into the distance before them.

Gibson led their pack-mule whilst Wall sat firmly on his saddle with his trusty scattergun across his waist. He was the eyes and ears of the three horsemen. The heavily built Texas Ranger looked out for any sign of danger that might arise and strike at them from any direction.

The three horsemen had made good time since leaving their Texan outpost.

They had managed to get through more than a dozen mounts between them on their long wearying quest.

A saddle-bag full of golden eagles had ensured that the three men could buy as much fresh horse-flesh as they needed to hasten their pursuit of the lawman they sought. It had proven an effective policy and the trio had managed to close the distance between themselves and Quaid from days to mere hours.

The soft sand beneath the hoofs of their horses began to slow their progress. Hume pulled back on his reins and stopped the tired mount beneath him. He slid off his saddle, crouched down and ran his gloved hand back and forth through the sand.

Wall and Gibson dismounted behind him and walked to the silent Texas Ranger officer.

'What's wrong, Cap?' Tanny Gibson asked.

Hume glanced up at the younger man and smiled. 'No trouble, Tanny. I just thought we'd make better pace if'n we take the saddles off our horses and let the poor critters rest for an hour.'

Gibson nodded and headed for their pack-mule.

Col Wall leaned on his scattergun and stared all around the moonlit landscape.

'We eatin', Matty?' he asked.

Hume rose to his full height.

'Reckon so, Col.'

'Break out some vittles, Tanny,' Wall told Gibson. 'We're gonna eat.'

Captain Hume exhaled heavily and rubbed his rump with both his gloved hands. It had been a long hard ride, and every bone in his body ached.

'You ever think about anything else but grub, Col?'

Wall smiled. His eyes twinkled in the moonlight.

'I thinks about females and beer! But most of all I thinks about vittles.'

Hume nodded and smiled.

'I don't cotton to being out on this damn prairie once the sun rises, Col. I figure we'll need every drop of our water just to survive this darn place.'

'How close do ya reckon we are to catching up with old Tom Quaid, Matty?' Wall asked, rubbing his belly.

'We're less than an hour or so behind the old-timer, Col.'

Wall leaned over and looked into the face of his superior.

'If'n we is that close to old Quaid, how come we're stoppin' for grub? We ought to ride hard and catch the old buzzard.'

Matty Hume pointed down at the tracks that led off into the eerie distance.

'That's why, Col.'

Col Wall removed his hat and scratched the top of his head as he stared down at the tracks.

'Huh? What ya trying to say, Matty?'

'Can't ya see it?'

'See what?' Wall shrugged.

Captain Hume shook his head. 'You'll never make a tracker, Col. Can't ya see the unshod hoof-tracks that have cut in from over yonder?'

Col Wall raised both his eyebrows.

'Unshod hoof-tracks?' he repeated. 'Are ya trying to tell me that them tracks are Injun pony-tracks?'

'Yep!' Hume sighed.

Tanny Gibson dropped the bag of food he had just pulled off the pack-mule on to the sand.

'Injuns?'

The Texas Ranger captain glanced at the youngest member of their small group.

'That's right, Tanny. We seem to have ourselves a whole bunch of Apache tracks here. Ya ain't worried, are ya?'

Tanny Gibson swallowed hard. He bent down and picked up the bag. His hands were shaking as much as his voice.

'Nope. Injuns don't bother me none, Cap,' he said. He straightened up with the bag in his arms again and walked towards the other two men.

Col Wall grabbed hold of Hume's arm.

'Exactly how many Injuns are we talkin' about, Matty? Ten? Twenty?'

'I figure that there must be at least fifty of the critters by the way the ground's all churned up, Col,' Hume replied, rubbing the back of his neck thoughtfully.

'Fifty?' Wall gulped. 'Fifty Apaches? That's an awful lot of Injuns. Are ya sure there's fifty?'

'Nope. I ain't sure. There might be maybe twice that many of them for all I know. It's hard to tell. The ground is kinda roughed up a tad,' Hume answered.

Tanny Gibson stopped in his tracks again and dropped the bag once more.

'How many?'

Wall spun on his heels and gazed around the horizon with increased alertness.

'Then how come we're stoppin' for vittles, Matty? We ought to be headin' after them critters before they catches up with old Quaid.'

'That's a hundred Apaches, ain't it?'

Tanny Gibson gasped in utter disbelief as he finally managed to calculate what double fifty was.

'Yep! About a hundred sounds right, Tanny.'

'We ain't got time to waste, Matty. Them Injuns will catch up with Marshal Quaid for sure. He needs our help. We can't leave him to get scalped,' Col Wall said.

Captain Hume shook his head slowly and pointed down at the sand again.

'They're ahead of Tom Quaid. Look at the sand, Col. The shod hoof-tracks are on top of the unshod ones. That means Quaid arrived here after the Apache rode through here.'

'Huh?' Wall was confused. 'What ya trying to say?'

'For some reason, the marshal arrived here trailing Diamond Back Jones and the bounty hunter them folks back at Dry Gulch told us about. I figure that Jones met up with his Apache kin and they gave chase to the bounty hunter. Marshal Quaid decided

131

to keep trailing them because Diamond Back is out there someplace.'

'How come they would chase the bounty hunter?' Wall asked.

'Iron Eyes is a strange dude. Outlaws hate his guts and so do the Apache.' Matty Hume sighed. 'For some reason they reckon that he's a living ghost or somethin'. He's killed his share of their tribe over the years and they might have thought about getting their own back.'

Gibson picked up the bag once again and brought it to the two men. He spoke reluctantly.

'Shall I fix a fire, Cap?'

'Yep. Use some empty flour-bags to make a fire, Tanny. There's plenty of dry brush around here to get a good blaze goin'. I want to drink me a couple of cups of coffee and fill my guts with some salt pork before we head on out again.'

Anxiously Col Wall bit his lip.

'So we ain't in no hurry then?'

Matty Hume looked at his friend. 'I ain't been in no hurry since I first set eyes on them tracks, Col.'

12

Lightning was still exploding in the skull of the emaciated figure as his feet somehow continued to take him along the black cave passage. His innards felt as though they were melting inside his lean frame and the sound of his pounding heart continued to haunt him. More dead than alive, Iron Eyes walked like a zombie in search of sanctuary, his long arms stretched out before him. Every fibre of his being screamed out for him to rest but he knew there could be no rest whilst the deadly snake-venom still surged through him.

Only instinct was driving the bounty hunter on through the dark cave tunnel now. Iron Eyes had no idea where he was or even if he were still somehow alive. There were no rational thoughts in the bounty hunter's fevered brain. Only agonizing pain. Step after step, he continued heading into the gentle breeze that drifted through the otherwise stale air.

He had determined to remain upright and keep walking until he eventually died or recovered his wits long enough to reclaim his mind again. The pain was worse than anything he had ever experienced before.

How many times had he been stabbed, shot by guns and bows in the past? So many times that only the scars that covered his body kept accurate records. But nothing had been as bad as the pain which had ensued after the sidewinder's fangs had sunk into his flesh.

The venom from the rattler's vicious bite still coursed through his frail body like acid burning through gun metal. He felt icy cold and yet sweat had drenched his long, heavy trail-coat and his trousers until he looked like someone who had been caught in a cloudburst.

Fever confused the tall man's usually

calculating mind until he no longer had any faith in anything except the cool draught on his face.

Was any of this real? he asked himself.

Iron Eyes continued to lurch forward, wondering if he might be caught in the middle of some horrific nightmare. One caused by drinking bad liquor or tainted water.

Could he trust any of this?

Every step that he took allowed pain to race through him unchecked. The entire cave was still in total darkness and yet his mind was filled with blinding lights that tortured his every movement.

Surely no nightmare could be this torturous, he thought.

Iron Eyes staggered from one side of the cave tunnel to the next as blood poured from the countless wounds which covered his thin body.

Yet he did not notice them.

There was nothing apart from confusion in his mind. Delirium fogged every thought a split second after the tall bounty hunter became aware of it.

With every beat of his racing heart, it got worse.

Iron Eyes felt the ground beneath his boots fall away sharply. Somehow he stopped himself from falling, his hands managed to reach to either side of the cave walls as he stumbled.

But there was no strength left in his arms.

He felt himself falling face first but could not work out how to move his arms in front of him to try and break the fall. The bounty hunter fell straight down into a black pit.

To his fevered brain this was just another nightmare.

Then his face hit the sand, hard.

His entire body shook as it crashed on to the floor of the cave tunnel. He just lay there, winded, unable to move any part of his spread-eagled body.

He was drowning in just two inches of soft sand.

Iron Eyes tried to breathe but could

not find any air. Only granules of fine sand filled his nostrils. He tried to force himself up but there was no power left in the long weak arms which lay at his sides.

Then a strange screaming seemed to reach his ears. Iron Eyes tried to open his eyes but the sand made it impossible. He heard his name being called out over and over again, then suddenly realized that the voice he heard so clearly was his own. Somewhere in the depths of his subconscious mind, he was screaming out at himself with a fury only he could muster.

Iron Eyes moved his hands and dragged them across the soft sand until they touched the sides of his head. His fingertips clawed at the sand to either side of his face until they touched his bruised and bleeding skin. He forced the fine sand away from his mouth and managed to tilt his head over on to its side.

At last his open mouth managed to find fresh air. He filled his lungs.

It tasted good.

Iron Eyes knew that he was still alive. Bruised and battered, but still somehow alive. He had to be. Only being alive could hurt this much, he thought. He turned the palms of his hands until they were facing down and then pushed at the sand with all his might.

Somehow he managed to force his lean frame off the sand and roll over on to his side. The cool air was much stronger now and made him recall why he was here at all. He shook his head and felt his mind clear slightly.

His bony fingers scraped the sand from his eyes and rugged features but he could still not glimpse any light. He spat at the darkness angrily. Then his left hand found the Apache water bag at his side. It was leaking.

He scooped the bag up.

The crude stopper was gone. Iron Eyes groped around him but the blackness hid the small stopper well. He lifted the neck of the water bag to his lips, swilled the sand from his mouth and then spat again.

He drank until he could no longer drink another drop.

Then he filled the palm of one hand with the cool liquid and washed the fine granules off his face. As the water trickled down his battered features he felt the cool breeze on his skin far more strongly than before.

I must be close to finding the way out of here, he told himself.

Iron Eyes ignored the burning pain inside his guts, staggered back to his feet and inhaled deeply on the fresh air which was drying the water droplets on his face. Suddenly he buckled and felt the water being rejected by his stomach. It gushed from his mouth like a fountain. The bounty hunter felt a little better.

He wondered if he had washed some of the poison from his system. Iron Eyes straightened up, raised the bag to his mouth and finished its contents before tossing it away. He no longer felt sick but the agonizing pain continued to tear through him as he groped his way along the narrow passageway of stone.

Iron Eyes could feel his head starting to throb again as the snake's poison attacked his senses once more.

With his long arms outstretched to protect him from the uneven cave walls, he continued to ignore his pain and headed toward the cool breeze.

For what seemed an eternity, the tall lean figure moved slowly along the tunnel that had been carved by nature itself aeons ago.

The only thing which kept him moving was the feeling of air on his face and exposed torso as his long coat-tails flapped at his sides.

His mind drifted in and out of consciousness but his feet continued to take one step after another as though driven by a more basic instinct.

The instinct of survival.

The bounty hunter knew that he had been moving ever downward since he had started out on his quest to locate the source of the gentle draught.

But even he had no idea of exactly how far down the inside of the sand-rock ridge he had come. The natural passageway had twisted and turned several times as the fevered man had descended deeper and deeper into it.

As Iron Eyes groped his way around a narrow corner, his tired burning eyes saw a shaft of moonlight ahead of him. It seemed to be coming up from the floor of the cave nearly twenty feet away from him and danced hypnotically over the rocky walls all around him.

At last! Iron Eyes sighed.

He stopped and leaned against the cool rock surface and tried to collect his thoughts. The snake's venom had made him see many things since the fangs had sunk into his flesh and he still doubted his sanity.

Was this real?

Had he finally reached his goal?

The sweat-soaked Iron Eyes closed his eyes and counted for a few seconds.

He then slowly opened them again and stared at the strange eerie light ahead of him.

That's real! he thought defiantly.

He forced his bedraggled body away from the cave wall and staggered towards the beckoning light. Iron Eyes was like a moth being drawn to a flame. He could not resist it after spending so many hours in total darkness.

At last! I've reached it at last! He sighed dragging his feet across the uneven surface of the cave floor. His battered body seemed to be moving faster than it had since he had first felt the jaws of the viper squeeze around his boot.

Panting with exhaustion Iron Eyes staggered toward the luring shaft of moonlight. Then, as he almost reached it, he stumbled and swayed from one leg to the other. There was a reason why the light seemed to be coming from the cave floor ahead of him.

The reason being that it actually was coming up from below the floor of the cave.

His eyes widened and gazed down into another massive hole filled with water as he felt himself losing his balance. He could see the mouth of the cave he had been searching for so desperately, far below him. Blue moonlight spilled into the cave, reflected off the water's surface and danced across the roof.

Iron Eyes felt himself falling through the air, falling into the light. He watched as the water below him came up to greet his body.

He closed his eyes and landed in the deep water. A million droplets of water raced into the haunting light above him as his body submerged into the ice-cold liquid. He frantically clawed at the water until he managed to find the surface again.

The pool of fresh water rippled against the back wall of rocks, then washed his lean body over the lip of the cave mouth. He felt himself roll over several times until a boulder and some dry brush stopped him.

Iron Eyes lay like a soaked rag-doll on his back, trying to inhale as much air as his lungs could take. The water had been a shock to him but it made him more alert. He blinked hard and then raised his left hand and pushed the long wet strands of hair off his face.

It took several seconds before he was able to see clearly again. The sight of the large bright moon high above him greeted him. He was about to move when something to his right caught his attention.

Iron Eyes moved his head slightly and stared through the brush at the Apache warriors who were arguing less than a hundred yards from where he was lying.

It suddenly dawned on the bounty hunter that he was not on the other side of the ridge as he had first thought. He was at the foot of the sand-coloured rockface almost directly below the cave mouth from where he had started.

Iron Eyes sighed heavily.

Damn!

13

The chief stared hard into the emotionless face of his brother and eventually
lowered his hooded eyes to the ground.
The ruthless Apache known to the
outside world as Diamond Back Jones
had won their battle of wills. Conchowata raised his hands to the rest of the
warriors who surrounded them and
muttered to them reluctantly under his
breath.

'My brother has seen the ways of our
bitter enemies and he fears none of our
gods. If he has the courage to climb up
to the cave and do battle with Iron Eyes
or the demons that might have already
destroyed him, let it be!'

Geroma stepped forward.

'But if our gods are upset, it shall be
we who pay, my father!'

Conchowata nodded.

'I have spoken.'

Diamond Back Jones pulled one of his guns from its holster and cocked its hammer until it locked fully into position. He glanced across the troubled faces of the other braves, then turned.

Like the Apache that he had always been, he moved like a mountain lion up the steep rugged rocks toward his goal. The moonlight still covered the warm face of the ridge and made the ascent easy for the agile figure.

Jones held the primed pistol in his right hand as he used the fingers of his left to claw at the rocks and assist his balance as he went swiftly higher and higher.

It seemed too easy for the deadly killer.

He knew that only a few hours earlier, the bounty hunter had used his high vantage point to shoot every one of the Apache warriors who dared to climb up towards the cave mouth, off the sand-coloured ridge.

Now there was no sign of the man who had become a legend in the hearts of the Indians. A man who had attained almost mythical prowess.

As Diamond Back Jones got within ten feet of the gaping cave entrance, he stopped and listened for any hint of movement above him.

There was nothing but silence.

Where was the man who, it was said, could not be killed because he was already dead? The outlaw began to move slowly up the narrow ledge again, with his gun aimed ahead of him.

He was waiting for any sign of the bounty hunter to emerge from the cave. Diamond Back Jones knew that Iron Eyes was faster than any other human being with his deadly Navy Colts. As he carefully edged his way up the rockface, he waited for the haunting figure to move out of the sanctuary he had found and start blasting with his guns.

Jones knew that he was dicing with death just trying to reach the cave. He had already witnessed the lethal accuracy of the bounty hunter's guns and knew that Iron Eyes had no gods

147

dictating to him when he could or could not kill his enemies.

Why had Iron Eyes not fired on him already?

Was he asleep?

Somehow the outlaw doubted that men like the infamous bounty hunter ever slept like other people.

Diamond Back wondered if some of the tall tales about Iron Eyes could actually be true. Was he a ghost who had been cursed to roam the plains until the end of time? Could he make himself invisible to the eyes of mere men?

There were still hours of the night left before the sun would eventually rise again. Yet, unlike the rest of his tribe, he was not willing to waste the entire night through fear of bringing the wrath of the gods upon them.

His time with the white men had made him impatient.

If Iron Eyes was still up there, he wanted to face him now and not wait until sunrise. If it meant dying, his

Apache blood did not mind.

For the Apache, like so many other tribes dotted across the vast continent, had a saying: it is a good day to fight, and a good day to die.

He would face his demons rather than cower from them like the rest of his people.

The outlaw leaned against the rockface and kept the barrel of his gun trained on the cave mouth, a mere six feet away from him.

He silently inhaled and gritted his teeth.

Diamond Back Jones leapt into the gaping hole in the rockface and rolled head over heels. As his boots landed on the sand, his left hand drew his other gun from its holster.

The cave floor was covered in blood.

Iron Eyes' blood.

But there was no sign of the bounty hunter.

Diamond Back Jones turned and looked down on his people.

'He has gone! Vanished!'

The Apache warriors mumbled amongst themselves as they watched the outlaw making his way back down the ridge towards them once again.

Perhaps Iron Eyes was a demon after all!

If so, how could they defeat him?

14

Tom Quaid pulled the black gelding up and stared into the moonlit panorama of high rocks which faced him. The ridge appeared to go on for ever in either direction. The sight that greeted his eyes chilled him to the bone.

He had never imagined in his wildest dreams that he would see so many Apache Indians in one place at the same time. Luckily for him, they had not noticed the mounted law officer on the prairie behind them. He thanked the Lord that the soft sand had muffled the hoofs of his long-legged black mount.

It had been a long ride to this remote place. Yet the trail had been an easy one for the marshal to follow. It had been littered with the bodies of Indians and ponies. The lawman had wondered how much of those bodies would be left once the sun rose and brought the vultures off the high peaks that surrounded the prairie.

He wrapped the reins around his saddle horn and quickly dismounted. His gloved hand grabbed the bridle and led the horse behind a broad Joshua tree. Sweat trickled down from the hatband of his Stetson over his weathered features as he unwrapped the reins again and looped them around the spiky trunk of the Joshua tree. His gloved hands knotted the leather firmly before he drew both his Remingtons and knelt down.

'I must be plumb loco!' Quaid scolded himself. 'I ain't no damn Indian fighter. What the hell am I doin' here?'

The Indians were looking up at something on the ridge but Quaid was too far away to tell what it was. He had no idea that Conchowata and his braves had been watching Diamond Back Jones returning along the steep ledge from the cave.

Tom Quaid began to speculate: could Iron Eyes have survived so many Apache braves and be cornered?

If the bounty hunter had survived, it must be some sort of miracle, the marshal thought. Quaid edged his way further around the thorn-covered bushes and squinted hard. Was Diamond Back Jones amongst those Apache braves?

He had to be! The marshal thought back to the trail he had so diligently followed to this spot. The hoof-tracks of Jones's horse had been easy to follow until the unshod mounts of the Indians had churned up the prairie sand. Then it was impossible to tell one set of tracks from another.

Quaid shook his head in frustration. Diamond Back Jones must be out there with those Indians, he thought.

But what if he wasn't?

How close to those painted warriors was he willing to get to find his man? He exhaled heavily and bit his dry lower lip. Even if the cold-blooded killer was with the rest of his people, how could he pluck Diamond Back Jones out of there without committing suicide in the process?

He rose slowly to his full height.

Now what did he do?

The question filled his tired mind. He had come so far following the outlaw who had killed his daughters. Quaid knew that he couldn't quit now.

Every fibre of what made him the man he was told him to mount up and hightail it out of here before the Apache spotted him and turned their rifles and bows on him. Yet he was haunted by the images of his children when he had discovered their bodies. Could he betray them?

Quaid knew the answer to that one. He could never quit until he had captured the outlaw who had ruined what was left of his life.

Was it vengeance that drove him on?

To Quaid it was more like retribution! He had to finish the job that he had started back in Waco. Whatever the cost, he had to see it through until the end.

He swallowed hard and studied the painted men. Quaid had never even met an Apache before let alone tried to fight a whole bunch of them. All he knew of the notorious tribe was what he had read in dime novels. How much of that was real and how much just the colourful scribblings of an army of Eastern writers?

There was no way of knowing.

All he knew for certain was that they had been trying to kill the bounty hunter and had lost scores of their own in the process. It had not seemed to trouble them, though. The Apaches appeared to be willing to sacrifice their lives in order to kill just one man.

In that way, they were very much like himself.

Quaid knew that made them a formidable enemy!

His eyes squinted into the moonlight and he hastily did a quick head count.

When he had reached sixty, he

stopped counting.

He felt sick.

This was not the way he had planned it. He had left Texas on the trail of one man, Diamond Back Jones. Along the tortuous trail he had learned many things about the wanted outlaw. The fact that Jones was actually a full-blooded Apache had not troubled him until this very moment.

He took another deep breath and tried to think.

It was pointless getting himself killed before he brought the outlaw to justice. Going anywhere near those Indians would prove fatal. Quaid knew he had to try to separate Jones from the rest of the Apache.

But how?

How was that possible?

If Diamond Back Jones was out there, he was using his entire tribe as a shield. The outlaw was every bit as cunning as the lawman thought him to be.

The marshal tried to think, but the

mixture of hunger and weariness made the task seem impossible.

Marshal Quaid gazed around the prairie. Apart from the sparse brush near the high wall of sandrock, there was little to hide behind.

Could one man take on so many? Again his thoughts drifted to the strange bounty hunter. Iron Eyes seemed to have survived against all the odds. He turned to his horse and looked at the Winchester in its leather scabbard, poking out from beneath the saddle fender. It might be possible to take the Apaches on if he could keep them at long range with his carbine, he thought. His mind raced as he vainly continued to try and make out Diamond Back Jones amongst the scores of painted warriors. Silently he cursed the light of the big yellow moon over his shoulder.

It played tricks on even the sharpest of eyes. Was the deadly killer he sought really there? If he was, Tom Quaid could not see him.

The marshal breathed out through his nostrils and listened to the sound of coyotes howling out across the arid prairie. Their howl was unlike that of other wild dogs. It had a way of chilling the souls of even the most determined of men.

Quaid straightened up and laid a gloved hand on the trunk of the Joshua tree. He wondered if he might have made a mistake out there on the trail as he followed the unshod hoof-tracks of the Indian ponies.

Maybe Jones had left the main group of riders long before reaching this place, he thought. Had his tired eyes actually missed the shod hoof-tracks of the outlaw's mount when it had ridden away across the sand?

Quaid had always prided himself on his tracking skills, but he knew that he was trail weary. He might have missed the telltale signs back there in the eerie light of the moon. Nothing seemed truly real any longer.

The marshal stared at the Apaches again.

Could he take on such a deadly force and then discover that the outlaw he sought had not even been with these lean near-naked figures in the first place?

Suddenly something caught his eye.

A glint of moonlight flashed out on the prairie as it danced off the long war lances of a group of silent riders. He turned his head and saw them.

His heart sank.

More Apache riders heading from the west towards the Indians gathered at the foot of the ridge.

Quaid holstered both his guns and moved slowly backward towards his horse. He turned and placed one hand on the black gelding's nose and pushed the animal as far into the tangled brush as it would go.

For some reason, sixteen more Apache riders were joining the main group.

Why?

What was going on?

Again Marshal Tom Quaid found

himself consumed by questions that had no answers. He held the nose of his mount firmly and whispered softly into the skittish animal's ear. He knew that if the innocent horse made just one sound, it would echo around the entire prairie and bring every one of those Apaches down on him faster than he could mount the gelding.

'Easy, boy!' he whispered over and over.

The lawman knew that he had ridden into something that he might live to regret. For the first time since he had headed out from Texas he began to wish that he had listened to his friends and allowed others to trail the outlaw.

He still wanted Diamond Back Jones more than life itself, but vengeance was a bitter pill to swallow when faced with such daunting odds.

For the first time in his long distinguished career the veteran lawman doubted his own judgement.

He rubbed the nose of the tall black

gelding and sighed heavily into its ear.

'We're in big trouble, boy! And I'm damned if I know how to get us out of it!' he admitted.

15

Iron Eyes was still in trouble. Big trouble. More dead than alive he still had enough spirit left to know that for the first time in all his days, he was staring into the jaws of death. The fever which had relentlessly consumed him for hours still raged inside his emaciated body. And yet he still could not work out why he was trapped in this devilish nightmare. Wisps of rational thought battled with the rattler's poison for control of what was left of his mind. He had always known that even the hunter must eventually face the Grim Reaper, but that did not answer the feverish question which tortured him.

How had he managed to get into so much trouble?

If there was an answer, it escaped him.

Iron Eyes had helplessly watched the

countless Apaches for what felt like hours as he lay soaked on his back in the dry brush outside the small cave opening at the foot of the ridge. The snake's poison still flowed through him unchecked and he had no idea how many times he had slipped in and out of consciousness since being washed out of the cave and into the dry undergrowth.

The bright moon still mocked his helplessness high above him and appeared not to have moved since his eyes had first looked up at it. Little time could have elapsed but Iron Eyes could not be certain of anything any longer.

Only the pain was real!

He tilted his head again and blinked hard trying to focus.

His small steel-coloured eyes trained on the growing number of Indians. Again he realized that he had not managed to escape them, but had actually been thrown to within a mere hundred or so yards from their camp-fires by the hidden cave pond.

His only hope of salvation was that they had not noticed him yet.

Iron Eyes had tried to move more than a dozen times since finding himself on his back outside the small half-hidden cave mouth.

Each time, the weak man had failed to even rise off his aching spine.

The bounty hunter wondered why more than a dozen Apache riders had joined the main group of warriors. He also wondered if even more of them might join the already formidable numbers.

What was going on?

Why were they so all-fired up?

Then he recalled all the times he had encountered the Apache warriors and how many of their tribe he had slain in combat. Yet Iron Eyes had never once killed an Indian who had not already tried to kill him first. There was no profit in killing men who had no bounty on their head.

But the Apaches had grown to hate him. His reputation had spread throughout their scattered tribes across hundreds of square miles.

He closed his eyes and tried to muster his flagging strength as he resigned himself to the fact that the Indian warriors would not rest until they had finally killed him. They wanted revenge and the name of revenge was Iron Eyes!

He raised his hands and slid them into the wet pockets of his drenched long coat.

Slowly his bony fingers searched the pockets for his guns and knife. Iron Eyes dragged them out and laid them on his bare bruised chest. He then searched for bullets but knew most of them had probably sunk to the bottom of the cave pool when he had fallen into its ice-cold water.

He managed to find just five of the .36 calibre bullets. He laid them at his side.

So few bullets and so many Indians, he thought.

The bounty hunter shook his head

and silently raged at himself. Iron Eyes twisted and slid the long blade of the Bowie knife into the neck of his left boot. Then his eyes studied the two wet pistols.

He knew that they were totally useless unless he could manage to dry them.

His long fingers opened the chambers of both Navy Colts and removed the bullets. Water ran freely out of the guns' innards and over his chest.

Iron Eyes was cursing with every frustrated movement of his bleeding hands. He grabbed the grips of the guns and shook them as hard as he could, trying to rid them of the water. He knew that he had lost his small toolbag containing the screwdrivers and oil required to clean the weapons. That had been in the saddle-bags of his injured pony back on the prairie.

The ice-cold eyes of the bounty hunter homed on to the guns with an intensity he had not been able to muster for hours. His mind raced.

Would his prized weapons work with

water inside their delicate insides?

There was only one way to find out and that was to load and fire them. That in itself would be suicidal.

He glanced again through the brittle brush at the Indians who were building their fires with every scrap of kindling that they could find. The entire rockface began to reflect the reddish hue of the flames.

Iron Eyes was troubled as he noticed the firelight dancing across him. He wondered how long he could remain undetected in this hiding-place.

Suddenly he felt the pain and fog returning to his weary brain. He inhaled deeply, then shook the delirium from his mind and pushed his damp limp hair off his face again. His eyes narrowed and stared hard at the two blue metal guns in his hands as they rested on his chest.

He looked for something to dry the pistols with. But it was a vain search as everything he wore was completely sodden.

The bounty hunter's eyes flashed again across at the scores of Apache braves who were milling around in total ignorance of his whereabouts.

Iron Eyes knew that if they caught even one whiff of his scent, he would most probably be dead within seconds.

There was an air of panic now racing through the outstretched figure as he felt the venom burning through him for the umpteenth time.

Somehow he had to dry his guns off.

Even if he managed to do so, he knew that there was no certainty that they would fire. Only once before in his life had he found his guns wet and it had taken two days before they had dried out well enough to fire.

Silently, Iron Eyes rolled over on to his belly.

He stared through the dry brush at the Indians again. For a few moments his eyes refused to focus, then he saw the figure in the Stetson. Instantly Iron Eyes recognized the outlaw known as Diamond Back Jones from their bloody encounter back in the remote town of Dry Gulch and the crude image that had adorned the wanted poster he had burned back in the cave tunnel.

The bounty hunter could almost taste the reward money in his cracked and bleeding mouth. He snorted quietly as anger welled up inside his lean frame.

Jones was so close and yet he might as well have been a thousand miles away for all the good it did Iron Eyes.

There was no way he could kill the outlaw now!

Not with so many Indians around and the uncertainty that his Navy Colts would not work whilst wet.

A lifetime of instinct made Iron Eyes want to kill the arrogant outlaw more than he had ever wanted to kill anyone before. Even in his confused state, he knew that the reward money on Diamond Back's head was more than generous.

But it had not been the money that had made him chase the outlaw with such determination. For all his reputation at being a heartless killer, he still had a hatred of anyone who harmed females. To him, it was something that no real man did.

To Iron Eyes, all outlaws were nothing more than animals that had gone mad.

He killed mad animals because they did not deserve to live amongst other creatures.

Diamond Back Jones was simply a two-legged mad animal that had to be destroyed.

It was a task Iron Eyes considered his duty.

Suddenly the pain increased and made the bruised and battered man clench both fists. He silently endured the agony that was slowly tearing him apart. His long body curled up and shook in uncontrollable spasms. Iron Eyes gritted his teeth and rode the demons inside his tortured carcass as if they were wild mustangs, until the horrific pain finally ebbed.

Exhausted, the bounty hunter felt his body relax.

He rubbed the sweat from both his eyes and looked at his guns again. He knew that without them, he was defenceless.

His hands clawed at the dry brush that surrounded him and he attempted to soak up the moisture from both the Navy Colts with the brittle grass.

There was no way of knowing whether it would work.

But he had to try.

After a few minutes he assembled the first of the guns and slid the bullets back into the chambers. Ten minutes later the second Colt was reassembled and loaded. A nagging thought returned to haunt him. Without oil on the dozens of springs and moving parts inside the pair of matched Colts, would they work when called upon to do so?

Iron Eyes rested his brow on the backs of his grazed hands and tried to find the strength that he knew had been sapped by the rattlesnake's vicious bite.

He raised his head slightly and stared across at the scores of Indian ponies that were within spitting distance of his hiding-place.

The trouble was, Iron Eyes had no spittle in his mouth. Only the acrid taste of poison that refused to go away. He breathed heavily, and slid his fingers around both his guns and cocked their hammers.

With every ounce of willpower that he could find in the depths of his soul, he forced himself up off the damp sand. He stood holding his guns in his hands and stared at the ponies.

Iron Eyes forced himself through the brush and staggered across the moonlit sand toward the ponies.

He was only half way when he heard the raised voices of the Apache warriors to his right. Scores of Conchowata's braves were racing across the distance between them.

Iron Eyes twisted his body, aimed and squeezed the triggers of both Navy

Colts at the fast approaching Indians.

Neither weapon fired!

Within a beat of his pounding heart, they were upon him!

16

To the injured bounty hunter it sounded as if the Devil had released untold numbers of demons from the very bowels of Hell itself to add even more pain upon his already half-dead body. Yet Iron Eyes knew that they were not creatures from another world, but his sworn enemy. His eyes widened as he saw the scores of knife-wielding Apache braves a moment before they over-whelmed him.

Iron Eyes crumpled under the sheer weight of the screaming warriors who had leapt upon him one after another. Yet even in his weakened state, it took more than a dozen of them to knock the staggering lean-framed man off his feet.

The vicious attack went on and on and yet they did not use the keen-edged blades of their knives on him. As the bounty hunter felt their fury, he wondered why they were only using their fists and clubs.

Any one of the painted braves could have used his dagger and ripped his heart out of his chest without him being able to prevent it.

Yet they seemed content to just batter him into a pulp.

Iron Eyes vainly tried to defend himself but it was impossible. There were simply too many of them to fend off. As one blow after another rained down on every inch of what was left of his body, he realized that he could not feel any of their punches or kicks.

The snake poison that coursed unchecked through his veins made him totally impervious to any exterior pain.

After being hauled back to his feet, Iron Eyes felt his body being dragged across the sand by countless hands. He knew that the Apaches had something planned for him but was helpless to stop them doing whatever they wanted.

His feet dragged behind him as the

Apaches brought him towards the largest of their campfires.

Blood was flowing from his scalp again and dripping from the long limp strands of his matted hair that hung above the moonlit sand. He tried to raise his head but could not.

Sweat dripped from his temples on to the sand almost as fast as the droplets of blood. He found himself staring at the strange pattern it made below him.

Even if he had been uninjured, the bounty hunter knew that he could not have withstood the strength of so many foes. More dead than alive, he had no chance.

His captors stopped and supported him between them as if he were little more than fresh game caught out on the prairie. It sounded to him as if every one of the Apaches was talking at exactly the same moment.

He could not understand one word of it.

Slowly Iron Eyes looked upward through his blood-soaked hair at the faces of the two men before him. Conchowata stood like a statue beside the raging fire. Its flames lit up the emotionless features of the Apache chief.

The grinning face of Diamond Back Jones looked exactly like the image on his wanted poster. The laughter of the outlaw made the bounty hunter fight against the numerous hands which held him in check.

It was a valiant but vain effort which only drained his strength even more.

'So this is the great Iron Eyes!' declared Jones as the warriors stood before him and the chief with their captive in their grip. He leaned closer and then spoke in English. 'I knew that you weren't indestructible, Mr Bounty Hunter! All them tall tales are nothin' but flannel, ain't they?'

'You reckon?' Iron Eyes asked through the blood that poured from his bruised mouth.

Diamond Back Jones moved forward and then kicked the belly of the tall man with all his might.

Iron Eyes was lifted off the ground by the sheer force of the kick. The Apache braves held his arms firmly so that he could not avoid Jones's second violent attack. This time the outlaw used the back of his right fist. It came down across the side of Iron Eyes' jaw, knocking the bounty hunter's head almost off his wide shoulders.

There was an eerie silence only broken by the chuckling of the Apache outlaw. He continued laughing until he saw the head of their captive defiantly rising until he was looking straight at Jones.

'I'm gonna kill ya, Jones!' Iron Eyes mumbled through his bloodstained teeth in a low growl. 'When this is over, I'm gonna kill ya good!'

The smile fell from the face of the outlaw as he stared into the cold eyes of the man before him.

'You kill me? When this is over, it'll be you who ends up dead, Iron Eyes. Not me.'

'Yep! I'm still gonna kill ya! Even if I have to do it after I'm dead,' Iron Eyes repeated slowly. 'I'll kill ya. That's a promise.'

Diamond Back Jones pulled one of his guns from its holster and aimed the barrel straight at the head of the dazed bounty hunter. He cocked its hammer.

'You ain't gonna kill nobody. Not if I blow ya damn head off, you ain't!'

Conchowata took a step and grabbed the outstretched sleeve of the outlaw.

'This is not the way, my brother!'

Diamond Back Jones swiftly turned his head and stared into the face of the chief. He could see the hooded eyes narrowing as they focused upon him.

'What?'

'You cannot kill him like this, my brother!' Conchowata said firmly. 'Not this way. That would be too quick. Iron Eyes must suffer for all the pain that he has inflicted upon our people. This is what we agreed. Do you not recall?'

Jones slowly released the hammer of his gun and lowered his arm. The gun slid into its holster silently.

'But we have him! We can kill him! Then it will be all over, great chief.'

Conchowata shook his head.

'Iron Eyes must die slowly, my brother. He will beg us to end his worthless life before we are finished torturing him. This day the Apache shall have their revenge on the living ghost.'

Iron Eyes had no way of knowing what the two men were talking about but knew that the outlaw was unhappy.

'Listen to ya chief, Jones! He's a lot smarter than you'll ever be.'

Diamond Back Jones clenched his fist and then violently punched the bounty hunter square on the jaw. The man's head rocked and then dropped until his chin hung over the sand. More blood flowed from the crimson-stained mouth.

Conchowata gestured to his braves.

'Bring the evil one to the fire. He must suffer a million deaths before we end his life.'

The muscular Indians dragged the helpless Iron Eyes across the sand to where their chief was pointing. The braves threw him down on to the sand.

'What ya intending to do to me, Chief?' the bounty hunter asked as he felt a dozen knife blades pressed at his throat and body. 'Ya boys here could have finished me off a score of times already. Ya planning somethin' special for old Iron Eyes?'

Conchowata stared grimly at their defiant prisoner. He was surprised by the sheer spirit and courage of their prisoner. He walked closer and then spoke in English.

'We shall skin you alive, Iron Eyes. Then we will cut your belly open and drag your worthless entrails out for the vultures to feast upon. Then after you have suffered the points of a hundred blades, we shall kill you.'

The bleeding figure of Iron Eyes nodded as the words sank into his fevered mind.

'Too much information, Chief!' he drawled. 'But I'm grateful for ya honesty.'

17

The sight which met the eyes of the weary lawman out on the prairie filled him with a mixture of horror and revulsion. For nearly an hour he had been wondering whether he ought to give up the idea of going anywhere near the scores of Indians, in the vain hope of finding, capturing or even killing Diamond Back Jones.

Now the sight that his weathered eyes focused upon in total disbelief gave him the spur that he needed to act. The Apaches had made up Marshal Tom Quaid's mind for him.

He swallowed hard and vainly tried not to watch the ungodly scene that unravelled before him.

Open mouthed, he watched the pitiful Iron Eyes being hoisted up on a crude wooden frame before the raging flames that licked at the moonlit sky.

Tom Quaid felt as if he were witnessing a latter-day crucifixion.

It chilled him to think that any man could be subjected to such barbaric torture. Yet he had seen many similar events in his long life and could not judge the Indians. They were simply doing what so many other people had done over the centuries. They were administering their own brand of justice.

There were no doubts left in the mind of the lawman. Now Quaid had no option but to help another helpless victim, as he had done so many times before. Forty years of upholding the law and protecting the innocent would not allow him to ride away from this. Even if he paid the ultimate penalty, he would have to try and save the man who was being tortured.

The marshal could not tell exactly how the Apaches had managed to attach their prisoner to the wooden frame, but that did not matter to the man who grabbed hold of his saddle horn and stepped into the well-used stirrup. As he sat across the wide back of his black gelding, Tom Quaid knew that he had at last found the reason he had been searching for.

The marshal tapped his spurs gently and allowed the tall horse to walk away from the Joshua tree and out into the brilliant moonlight.

He gritted his store-bought teeth and narrowed his determined glare at the distant scene beneath the wall of sand-rock. Giant shadows loomed across the face of the wall of rock as the dancing braves circled the well-fed fire and their half-dead captive.

The marshal noticed the mist drifting across the wide moonlit prairie. Yet the jubilant Apaches seemed oblivious to everything except the task in hand. Quaid glanced up at the sky above him and inhaled deeply. Black clouds were now tracing across the heavens from the east.

He wondered if they might give him the cover he required to get closer to the chanting warriors. Black shadows swept over the flat prairie as the clouds passed before the face of the bright moon.

Was this a sign for him to drive his spurs into the flesh of his faithful mount and charge at the countless Apaches? The thought lingered in his mind.

For several minutes the lawman sat astride his mount watching the Indians as they secured the twisted wooden frame into the soft ground. Yet still none of them noticed the elegantly dressed marshal who observed them.

The triumphant war cries that echoed out across the vast prairie told Quaid that the Indians had only one thought in their collective mind.

And that was to torture their prisoner in ways that even he could not imagine.

A solitary bead of sweat trickled down from the hatband of his Stetson and navigated every one of the tanned wrinkles which covered his ancient face. Finally it dripped from his solid chin and landed on the back of his left gloved hand which rested on the saddle horn.

Those dime novels he had read with such relish for so many years were nothing compared to the gory reality that faced him now.

No Eastern writer, however imaginative, could have conceived of such horror, he thought.

There was something terrifying about the sound of so many dancing Apaches chanting their songs of victory which chilled the old horseman.

He edged his horse closer and closer to the scene ahead of him trying to see if the long-haired man who was somehow tethered to the crude wooden crucifix was still alive.

The light of the Apache camp-fire illuminated the man in every detail. As Quaid's mount got ever closer, it became obvious that their victim was indeed alive. Even covered in enough blood to give the appearance that he had been painted, the man on the wooden frame was still capable of moving his head.

Quaid felt a lump in his throat.

At first the marshal wondered if it was Diamond Back Jones who had been hoisted into the air. It was the long dark hair that fooled the curious onlooker. Then Tom Quaid pulled back on his reins and swallowed hard.

He knew that Jones, like most Apaches, was only a little more than five feet in height.

The man who was naked apart from the torn bloodstained trousers and boots, had to be well over six feet in height.

'Iron Eyes!' Quaid said under his breath. 'That poor bastard has to be Iron Eyes!'

A fury suddenly exploded inside the innards of the veteran peace officer. He watched as Iron Eyes' head lifted up and stared beyond the black clouds at the bright moon over the prairie as if searching for a god that might send some guardian angel down to help him.

Quaid wondered if *he* might be Iron Eyes' guardian angel! Had the fates or something else brought him to this spot simply to bring salvation to the bounty hunter?

Marshal Tom Quaid had not even waited long enough to hear the preacher's words at his own daughters' joint funeral service back in Waco. He had lost his faith the day he had discovered their bodies, had thought that nothing could make him even consider that there might be something he could pray to ever again.

Had he been wrong?

Could it have been providence and not vengeance which had brought him here?

As the marshal watched the long sharp points of the war lances being poked into the flesh of the helpless bounty hunter, he realized that there had to be some higher meaning to all of this.

Quaid pulled the reins up and then looked back at the brush which surrounded the Joshua tree. It was kindling-dry. He had an idea.

He hauled the head of the horse around and then rode back to the place where he had hidden for so long as his confused mind tried to work out what he ought to do.

Tom Quaid stopped the gelding and glanced briefly across at the Indians again. They still had not noticed his presence.

As mist rolled over the moonlit ground, the determined marshal wrapped his reins around the saddle horn, then pulled his frock-coat away from the silk vest. His gloved fingers found the large silver cigar-case in the pocket over his heart. He withdrew it.

With one eye on the chanting braves, Quaid carefully opened the silver lid of the case and removed a cigar. He placed it between his teeth and then pulled out a long match from a special compartment inside the case.

He struck the match and inhaled the strong smoke deeply before cupping the flame and tapping his spurs until the black gelding moved close to the dry brush.

Tom Quaid knew that to get close enough to the bounty hunter in order to try and rescue him, he had to cause a distraction. A fire would be made to order.

It might buy him enough time to circle the Indians and get in behind them. All he had to do was distract enough of the Apaches long enough for him to gallop to the aid of Iron Eyes. He knew that it was probably doomed to failure, but he had to give it a try.

Just as he was about to throw the burning match into the bushes, he saw something riding towards him through the mist and murky light of the moon.

There were three riders with a pack-mule.

Marshal Tom Quaid lifted the match to his mouth and blew its flame out.

He inhaled the smoke again and then removed the cigar from his lips. As more and more dark clouds raced across the face of the moon, his eyes darted back and forth between the raging Apaches to the approaching horsemen.

He rested the palm of his gloved right hand on the grip of the Remington in its holster and then felt himself suddenly relax.

'What in tarnation is Matty Hume doing here?' he asked himself quietly. 'Not like him to get lost.'

The three Texas Rangers continued to ride towards the lawman, unseen by the celebrating Apaches.

'We've bin lookin' for ya, Tom,' Col Wall said. The three riders stopped their mounts beside the marshal's horse at the Joshua tree.

Quaid nodded as smoke drifted from his mouth.

'I hate to upset you boys, but this ain't Texas.'

Matty Hume stared through the dry brush at the scene of brutality near the ridge.

'What's goin' on over yonder, Tom?'

The lawman glanced to where Hume was pointing before returning his attention to his friend.

'Them Apaches have got themselves a prisoner, Matty! His name's Iron Eyes, I think. I was just about to try and rescue the critter.'

Wall sighed.

'Are ya loco? There must be nearly a hundred Injuns over there. What was ya gonna do, Tom? Surround the varmints?'

Quaid looked at the pack-mule thoughtfully.

'Have you boys got any dynamite on that animal?'

Hume nodded, then smiled.

'We happen to have a few sticks. Reckon ya thinking the same way as me, Tom.'

The marshal tapped the ash from his cigar.

'Do you want to help me save a critter from being tortured to death, Matty?'

Hume looked into the faces of his

two companions. They averted their eyes from the horrific scene and looked straight at their captain.

'Should we help this old rooster, boys?'

'I'm game!' Tanny Gibson nodded firmly. 'I can't leave no man to them merciless Apaches, Cap. We gotta help.'

Hume looked at Wall.

'What about you, Col? You figure we ought to give this old Texas lawman a helping hand?'

Col Wall's eyes sparkled in the moonlight.

'Sure enough, Matty. I ain't got nothin' else to do but I still figure we might be bitin' off more than we can chew.'

Hume raised an eyebrow at his well-built friend. A man with an appetite as big as the broad smile that never seemed to fade.

'More than you can chew? There ain't no such animal, Col.'

Marshal Tom Quaid leaned across toward the three nervous Texas Rangers and began to speak.

'Listen up, boys. This is my plan . . . '

18

The explosion was big and unexpected by all, except the four riders who raced in all directions from their first well-placed dynamite stick. There was nothing left of the Joshua tree or any of the dry brush which had surrounded its spiky trunk. Just a burning scar on the blackened sand. Debris had flown into the air as the shock waves expanded out from the nucleus of the explosion.

The three Texas Rangers and the marshal had waited until a large black cloud had moved between the bright moon and the land beneath its eerie light before they acted.

The fuse had been trimmed short.

Real short.

It had taken less than a minute for it to burn down to the detonation cap that was rammed into the soft dynamite stick. But it had been enough time for the quartet of horsemen to ride wide of the Apaches' camp-fire.

Iron Eyes had thought that the snake-venom and cruel points of the Indians' sharp lances were making him hallucinate once more. There had been so many nightmares for the bounty hunter since he had last managed to sleep.

He had watched the four riders in the distance for what had seemed an eternity from his painful vantage point high on the face of the crude wooden torture rack.

As the power of the explosion rocked him, he began to realize that this was actually real. The attention of the Apaches was suddenly drawn away from their prisoner and aimed at the distant flames.

It was a confused Iron Eyes who watched as the stunned painted warriors raced to their lines of ponies. He could still feel the shock waves rocking the high pole he was tethered to, as they bounced off the ridge behind him.

The eyes of the bounty hunter darted from one outstretched arm to the other. The Indians had done a good job binding his wrists and biceps to the long twisted crossbar. He was hanging like meat in a butcher's shop.

They had used wet rawhide which was designed to tighten as the moisture evaporated from it.

Now after more than an hour the rawhide had shrunk to half its original size and was cutting into his flesh.

His weary eyes could see blood starting to weep from the leather restraints. Yet there was no pain. He had not felt any of his enemies' brutal attacks since they had eventually caught him near their mounts. The poison in his body ensured that nothing else could hurt him.

Iron Eyes stared around the vast mist-covered prairie trying to see the four horsemen again. He could not.

Conchowata and Diamond Back Jones had not moved away from the massive camp-fire with the rest of their fellow Apaches and were now the only braves to remain near their precious prisoner. Yet all thoughts about Iron Eyes had evaporated as their attention was drawn to the prairie.

The half-dead bounty hunter watched as the screaming Apaches rode their ponies out towards the still burning hole in the sand where the four Texans had blown up the undergrowth. He wondered who they were and why they had acted.

Were they trying to help him? If so, why?

The tortured man lowered his chin and stared down at the two men below him. If he were ever going to act, he knew that it had to be now!

He leaned forward and felt the pole move in the soft sand far below him. Then he rocked back. Every sinew in his body screamed out for him to stop, but he could not. Somehow Iron Eyes managed to make the wooden pole respond to his slightest change of weight distribution.

The pole was moving a few inches at first and then more and more as the man strapped to it found hidden reserves of strength somewhere within his determined spirit.

No fear existed in his lean blood-covered frame as he managed to get the pole rocking back and forth with more rapidity. All he could think about was making the base of the pole either snap or topple out of the soft sand.

But it was a risky business.

Iron Eyes knew that if it did fall forward he would more than likely land in the flames of the Apaches' massive camp-fire, yet he was unafraid.

Suddenly another massive explosion erupted near the still-smouldering hole out on the scarred prairie. The Texas Rangers had left three more sticks of dynamite with various lengths of lit fuses.

As the scores of Apache horsemen had neared the site of the first explosion, the second stick had gone off. Riders and ponies were thrown into the air as the lethal dynamite erupted into action.

Then another stick violently blasted and then the fourth.

It was carnage!

More than half the Apaches were either dead or maimed by the force of the three later explosions. Those who were left of the painted riders were stunned and half-blinded by the unexpected blasts.

As the remaining Apaches managed to regain control of their ponies, they suddenly heard the sound of rifle shots echoing out around the immense prairie.

The trio of Texas Rangers had used the shadows of the storm clouds well. They had managed to fan out into the mists that drifted over the ground to their advantage. Now they were attacking with their long rifles in their experienced hands as their legs guided the well-trained mounts beneath them.

The Apache horsemen were in a turkey-shoot, and it was they who were the targets of the skilled riflemen.

Iron Eyes could see every single detail of the battle that was raging far beyond him. He continued to rock the pole that he was strapped to as he noticed the Apache chief being drawn further and further away from him.

Chief Conchowata looked in horror at his warriors being killed and knew that he could do nothing about it. The Apache leader ran to his pony, leapt across its back and then galloped off towards the raging battle. He knew that he would probably not survive, but he chose to fight and die with his braves.

Diamond Back Jones drew both his Colts from his holsters and cocked their hammers. Unlike the rest of his tribe, he had no sense of honour or loyalty. He knew that he now had to escape from the unexpected mayhem.

Jones was just about to approach his own horse when he heard the creaking of the pole behind him.

With the speed of a puma, he spun on his heels and looked at their prisoner. The face of Iron Eyes was without expression as he forced the pole forward for the last time.

There was a loud cracking sound at the base of the pole. It seemed to shudder as it tumbled with its helpless victim tied to its frame.

Jones moved toward the fire and aimed both pistols into the air. But the pole was falling faster than even he could squeeze his triggers.

A million burning splinters rose into the air as Iron Eyes disappeared into the flames.

The Apache outlaw fired over and over again into the inferno before him as he tried to approach the hot blinding wall of fire that spewed burning debris in all directions. Jones knew that the bounty hunter had been engulfed by flames and there was no escape.

Before Jones could holster his guns, he felt the gun in his left hand being torn from his grip as the deafening sound of a bullet crossed the distance between the approaching rider and the outlaw.

Diamond Back Jones turned and looked straight at the black gelding which was galloping toward him. The star of the lawman flashed in the firelight.

The outlaw cocked the hammer of his remaining Colt and then quickly fired at the marshal.

Tom Quaid felt his faithful mount collapse beneath him. He flew helpless through the air and crashed into the soft forgiving sand. He rolled over several times before finding himself at the feet of the outlaw.

Jones laughed as he cocked the hammer of his gun and aimed it at the head of the dazed marshal who was lying on the sand.

'Looks like it's my lucky day, Marshal Quaid!' The outlaw grinned as he closed the distance between them. 'First I gets to see old Iron Eyes killed and now I gets to kill you.'

Tom Quaid blinked hard and stared

into the barrel of Jones's primed pistol.

'Shoot, ya bastard! Kill me like ya killed my daughters!'

Diamond Back Jones grinned even wider.

'Was them your daughters? They was sweet. Never tasted sweeter, Marshal! It was a shame to kill them afterwards, but they was sort of messed up. I figured it would be kinder to put the bitches out of their misery!'

Furiously, Quaid felt himself rising off the sand. The outlaw's gun fired and a bullet caught him in the shoulder. But the lawman still came up off the sand at the outlaw.

'I'm gonna kill ya, Jones!'

Quaid's hands grabbed at the throat of the Apache outlaw, who began to cock his pistol once again. The marshal felt the cold barrel of the weapon push into his belly as he squeezed Jones's throat with every ounce of his being. If he couldn't get a noose around Jones's neck, he'd do the job with his fingers, he silently vowed.

Then as their faces were just inches apart, Quaid felt the outlaw shudder. Diamond Back Jones's eyes widened and he dropped the gun. The marshal continued to throttle the man in his grip until he realized that the outlaw was somehow already dead.

A confused Quaid released his grip. The lifeless outlaw fell in a heap at the marshal's feet.

Tom Quaid narrowed his eyes and saw the long Bowie knife in the back of the outlaw lying before him. He blinked hard again and lifted his head. He stared in disbelief at the horrific image of Iron Eyes staggering away from the flames of the campfire towards him.

He had never before seen anyone still somehow alive who looked quite as dead as the bounty hunter did.

It seemed impossible to the marshal that anyone could have survived falling into such a ferocious fire as the one the Apaches had made. Yet Iron Eyes was staggering across the scorched, blood-stained sand defiantly.

The bounty hunter was burned beyond description. Smoke drifted off every part of him. Only his long sweat-sodden hair remained untouched by the fire he had fallen into.

Iron Eyes bent down and dragged his knife out of the body and tucked it back into his smouldering boot.

'They never even thought that I might have me a knife tucked into my boot,' Iron Eyes said wearily.

'Are you OK, son?' Marshal Quaid heard himself ask the ridiculous question.

Iron Eyes looked at the triumphant Texas Rangers who were headed towards them. He then glanced back at the lawman.

'I've bin better, old man!'

Finale

The Texas Rangers had managed to survive their battle with the Apaches out on the prairie but they knew that without the four sticks of deadly dynamite, it would have been a very different story indeed.

To their utter amazement, Conchowata had fearlessly ridden into the hail of Winchester bullets and guided what was left of his defeated tribe away to the safety of the mists that continued to trace their way across the moonlit sand.

Matty Hume, Col Wall and Tanny Gibson had allowed the Apache chief safe passage until he and his surviving braves had headed back into the uncharted territory which had spawned them. The Texas Rangers had no desire to kill any more of their worthy opponents and were grateful that luck had been on their side.

But it was the scene that greeted them when they had followed Tom Quaid's trail to beneath the ridge which had taken them by surprise.

None of the three horsemen had expected to set eyes upon anything quite so gruesome as the sight of the badly injured Iron Eyes, who had saved the wounded marshal. As a few rays of light moved across the sky signalling an end to the seemingly eternal night, Iron Eyes totally ignored them.

Col Wall had started to use the dying embers of the Indians' fire to rustle up some breakfast.

'Ya hungry?' Wall had asked the bounty hunter.

'Got any whiskey?' Iron Eyes responded.

'Nope. But I got bacon, and flour to make biscuits.' Wall smiled.

Iron Eyes shook his head and continued to roam around searching for anything that he might be able to use on his long journey away from this place. He managed to locate the handful of .36 calibre bullets he had lost in his struggle with the Apaches and tucked them into his trouser pockets.

'Reckon that reward money will buy ya plenty of whiskey, Iron Eyes,' Tanny Gibson commented.

Iron Eyes spat at the ground and growled.

'I don't want no reward money off that critter, sonny. The marshal can have the carcass.'

Matty Hume studied the tall man carefully as he finished tending to the wounded marshal. He had cleaned the bullet hole as best he could and then made a sling for Quaid's arm.

'Reckon that varmint is ready to drop, Tom.'

Quaid nodded.

'That's what I was thinkin', Matty,' the marshal agreed. 'I just don't understand how he ain't already dead.'

'Maybe he is!' Hume sighed.

Tom Quaid picked up the two matched Navy Colts from the sand, then managed to muster the nerve to approach the tall severely burned man who could no longer hide the pain that was consuming him.

'Can we talk, Iron Eyes?'

The bounty hunter led Diamond Back Jones's mount away from the remnants of the camp-fire and picked up his long coat from the sand. He slipped it over his blistered skin and accepted his two prized Navy Colts from the frowning lawman.

'Talk, old man!'

'You could come back to Waco with us, Iron Eyes,' Quaid said. He opened the silver lid of his cigar-case and offered the bounty hunter the last of his expensive smokes.

Iron Eyes slipped the guns into his deep coat pockets and accepted the cigar. He pulled his long knife from his boot and carefully cut the cigar into two equal portions.

Tom Quaid accepted the half cigar and placed it between his lips. He watched Iron Eyes grip his with his small teeth.

The marshal struck a match and lit both their smokes.

'Well?'

'I never cottoned to Waco, Marshal,' Iron Eyes said as he stepped into the stirrup and hoisted his body on to the back of the outlaw's horse. 'Besides, I reckon I've got me a longer journey to negotiate.'

Quaid looked at the man hard. Blackened skin was peeling from Iron Eyes' body as he gathered up the reins and sucked on the strong cigar.

'You need them wounds tended, son!' Quaid said. 'Let me and the boys help ya.'

Iron Eyes was silent. He could still feel the venom of the rattlesnake burning at his guts. He gripped the saddle horn and felt himself leaning forward as the pain grew more intense inside him.

'Look at me, Iron Eyes!' Marshal Quaid insisted as he watched the man above him fighting the agony he was now unable to hide from the four onlookers. 'If you don't let us help ya, you'll more than likely die! You was snake bit, boy! Snake bit and God only knows what else.'

'So?' Iron Eyes gripped the cigar hard.

'You could die!' Quaid repeated.

Iron Eyes exhaled a cloud of smoke and then nodded at the concerned lawman. His face was etched by pain.

'Too late, Marshal! Reckon ya a tad too late!'

The Texans watched silently as the bounty hunter tapped his spurs into the flesh of his newly acquired horse and rode away from them.

The lone rider headed straight into the rising sun, leaving the four Texans to wonder what he meant. With every stride of his horse's long legs, Iron Eyes slumped further over the neck of the mount.

As the blinding light of a new day engulfed the prairie, Iron Eyes was gone.

We do hope that you have enjoyed reading this large print book.

Did you know that all of our titles are available for purchase?

We publish a wide range of high quality large print books including:
Romances, Mysteries, Classics
General Fiction
Non Fiction and Westerns

Special interest titles available in large print are:
The Little Oxford Dictionary
Music Book, Song Book
Hymn Book, Service Book

Also available from us courtesy of Oxford University Press:
Young Readers' Dictionary
(large print edition)
Young Readers' Thesaurus
(large print edition)

For further information or a free brochure, please contact us at:
Ulverscroft Large Print Books Ltd.,
The Green, Bradgate Road, Anstey,
Leicester, LE7 7FU, England.
Tel: (00 44) **0116 236 4325**
Fax: (00 44) **0116 234 0205**

Other titles in the
Linford Western Library:

COLD GUNS

Caleb Rand

A few years after the Civil War, Lou Hollister returns to Texas, bearing the cruel scars of an enemy prison stockade. Once home, he thinks he can settle and cast off a beleaguered past. Instead, he finds a family without hope, and a ranch manipulated by Tusk Tollinger, the corrupt sheriff of Cottonwood County. Lou fights to regain his ranch, and when a great snowstorm surges in from the Sacramento Mountains, he must confront his tormentors from the past. Can he now wreak his final, bloody revenge?

HIGH STAKES SHOWDOWN

Mike Redmond

The placid work routine at the Ferguson Ranch is abruptly shattered one afternoon when young cattleman Matt Farrell discovers a dead body on the range and simultaneously finds himself at odds with the foreman, McCoy, over the favours of old Ferguson's feisty daughter, Hetty. Now a breathless sequence of events finds Farrell braving a lynch mob, defending himself in a brutal bare-knuckled fight and facing death in a final shootout in a spooky Arizona ghost town . . .

THE GUN MASTER

Luther Chance

They lived in the shadow of a fear that grew by the hour, dreading the moment when their world would be destroyed by a torrent of looting and murder. And when that day finally dawned, the folk of Peppersville knew they would be standing alone against the notorious Drayton Gang. There was not a gun in town that could match the likes of the hard-bitten, hate-spitting raiders. But now it looked as if change was on the way with the arrival of the new schoolteacher, the mysterious McCreedy . . .

KINSELLA'S REVENGE

Mark Falcon

Newton, Kansas, was a cow town in 1871, when bounty hunter twin brothers Fin and Ray Kinsella became involved in what was to be called 'the Newton General Massacre'. It was to lead Ray on the road to revenge. Along the way, Ray and the three-man posse met up with Kitty Brown, sole survivor of a family murdered by one of the men they were tracking. She joined the posse on a ride that would change all their lives. And, when the shooting stopped, revenge from beyond the grave would come to haunt them all.